THE DEVIL'S HEART
DARK TIDES

BOOK ONE

By
Candace Osmond

CANDACE OSMOND

Cover Work by Majeau Designs
Facebook.com/MajeauDesigns

DEDICATION

To Corey, my heart.

ACKNOWLEDGMENTS

I always thank my cover designer, Majeau Designs. But a *thank you* simply isn't enough this time around. The cover for The Devil's Heart is nothing short of a work of art.

I also have to thank my readers for graciously accepting me back into the world of Paranormal Fantasy after I took a vacay in Thriller land.

CHAPTER ONE

I never gave much thought to whether magic actually exists. But sometimes you just can't ignore the weird occurrences that weave their way into our lives. Like Deja vu or unexplainable coincidences.

Or the cold, stark feeling you get when you *know* something bad is going to happen. The goosebumps that scrape across your skin and the heavy pit that touches the bottom of your stomach like a bag of ice.

The same feeling that currently inhabited my body. I felt the insistent vibrations of my cellphone pressing against my thigh. Nothing marked the day different from any other. But that first initial vibration, that first ring letting me know a call was coming through... it shook something inside me.

Only darkness awaited me on the other end.

I slipped a hand into my jeans pocket and pulled out my phone. The area code number on the screen verified my otherworldly hunch. With a deep breath, I tapped the green button.

"Uh, hello?"

"Dianna, m'dear!" The old raspy voice on the other end sounded familiar, and my mind scrambled to place it. "You're a hard girl to track down."

That ice-cold pit in my stomach felt like a frozen anvil as the cogs finally clicked in my brain. "Oh, hey, Aunt Mary. How's it going?"

"Oh, m'love, not good." My great aunt let an empty pause hold the line. Finally, I heard her inhale. "I imagine you know why I'm calling?"

I closed my eyes and tried to focus on breathing. "It's Dad, isn't it?"

"Yes, dear, he passed away yesterday afternoon. Poor soul."

I pressed my back against the bedroom wall and let the weight of my body slide its way down to the floor where I curled into a crouching ball, still holding the phone to my ear. I tried not to let the sounds of crying or the sudden dry tightness in my throat come through in my words. I didn't want to show weakness during the moment I'd been expecting for years.

My relationship with my father wasn't exactly warm and loving. He was a cold and distant man, drifting further and further away from me as the years went on. He called once a year, at Christmas, just to check in. Three years ago, however, he told me that he was dying. Cancer had found its way into his body and the doctors said it was only a matter of time. I was honestly surprised he hung on that long.

"Cool, okay." I fought for words. "Thanks for letting me know, Aunt Mary." Shakily, I stood up, cleared my throat and wiped my eyes, determined to keep it together. I would *not* cry for that man.

"Are you comin' home for the funeral? It's on Friday."

Just barely two days from now. I cringed when my brain immediately thought of how much work I had to do. Not exactly what someone should worry about when a parent dies. "Well -"

"Now you listen here," my aunt began to scold, her thick Newfoundland accent coming through in the hardest way, something that usually happened when we were either angry or drunk. I strained to make out all the words. "I know you and your father had a rough time since your mom died. But that's no excuse."

"I know, but Aunt Mar -"

"No buts!" She cut me off, making me feel like a child again. But I could hear her relax with the heavy exhale that came through the phone.

"Dianna, he's your *father*. He was devastated when your mother died. He lost the love of his life."

My free hand clenched into a tight fist and strained against the denim on my thigh. "I was a child, Mary. He shut me out. Yeah, he lost her… but so did I." I let that stew. "I loved dad, you know that. But I'm here in Alberta now, and I have a life. A *real* life. The restaurant just promoted me to sous chef and-"

"Dianna, you can cook in any bloody restaurant in the country. There will always be time for that. Besides, I need help going through their stuff. You're the last living heir to it all, you know that, right?"

I choked down the bubble that suddenly formed in my throat. "You mean… he left it all to me?" I hadn't even considered that possibility. My parents weren't rich, by any means. They owned a quaint little bakery that barely got by during the Winter months but thrived in the Summer, during tourist season.

But I wasn't thinking of that.

We have a strong Newfoundland bloodline that came over from England and Scotland, one that dated back to the 1600s. We had numerous properties; some old, some new, some so old they should have been torn down decades ago. But I remembered my mother collecting dozens of old trunks and antiques that had been passed down through generations.

Stuff from my dad's side and hers. Stuff that I was obsessed with as a kid. Swords, books, jewelry, and even pirates' chests. Well, what I *thought* were pirates' chests at five years old. Regardless, there were definitely things I wanted before the vultures of my distant family came and picked over the flesh. If Dad had left it all to me, that at least bought some time before things began to go missing.

"Fine, I'll make arrangements and come home for a few days." I regretted the words before I finished saying them. But it *was* my weekend off, so all I had to do was find someone to cover a couple of shifts until then. "But that's all I can do."

"Wonderful," Mary replied, "Call me when you get your flight booked. I'll come pick you up."

I let out a deep sigh. "Thanks, Aunt Mary. Bye."

I hung up the phone and slipped it back into my jeans pocket. The warm morning sun seeped in through the partially closed window blinds, casting an eerie yellow and grey striped pattern across my dark bedroom. I forced a smile on my lips as the man-shaped lump in my bed rolled over to face me.

"Hey, babe," he said in a creaky morning voice that was low and sexy. I watched his lean muscles flex with slight movements as he rubbed his tired face. I'd been dating John for a year now and things were finally starting to get serious. "Everything okay?"

"Yeah. I mean… no, not really." I paused to push those tears back in once again. "My dad died yesterday. That was my aunt calling."

He immediately sat up in bed, the thin grey sheet pooling around his waist. "Jesus, Dianna, are you alright?"

A slightly shaky nod was all I could afford. John outstretched his arms, inviting me back to bed. I had been on my way to work when Aunt Mary called. But, given the circumstances, I should take today off, too. Using my father's death as an excuse to get out of work seemed wrong to me, but it's what normal people would do, isn't it? Normal daughters, who knew how to sort through their feelings when a parent dies? I worked my ass off for that sous chef position at the restaurant, but they couldn't deny me a couple of days leave for this.

I crawled up the side of the bed and into John's warm embrace. The heat from his sleeping body still held within the blankets. I let it soak into my skin and inhaled the scent of him.

"I should call work and let them know. I'm going to try to get a flight for tomorrow." I stretched my neck, so my lips touched his soft mouth as I pulled my cell phone from my pocket one more time. But John snatched it from me.

"I'll call. Judy loves me."

It was true. My boss adored John. And, to be honest, who didn't? He's gorgeous, friendly, smart, and butters her up every chance he gets. I hate to think it had anything to do with me getting the promotion, but it probably did. Regardless of how hard I worked to get there.

I rested my head on his chest, in the crook his shoulder made for me when his one arm held me tightly. He quickly found the restaurant number in my contacts and then placed the phone to his other ear. In the silence of my bedroom, I could hear a few rings go in before someone picked up.

"Hardware Grill, Emily speaking. How may I help you?"

"Hey Em', it's John. Can I speak to Judy, if she's free?"

"Oh, hey John!" Emily's annoying voice reached the same squealy octave most girls' did around my boyfriend. "Sure, she's right here." I listened as my co-worker passed the phone over, light muffled sounds coming through.

"Hello?"

"Good morning, Judy, sweetheart," John schmoozed. "How's it going?"

"Oh, you know. Same ol', same ol'," my boss replied. "How are you, dear?"

"I'm good, sweets. But I'm calling on behalf of Dianna."

"Oh? Is she sick?"

"No, there's been a death in her family, so she needs three days bereavement plus her usual weekend. Is that okay? I'm sure you ladies can manage without her for a bit, right?" That's why I adored him. He had a way with words. Somehow, already getting the answer he wanted before the other person could even formulate one.

"Oh, well, um," Judy stammered over her thoughts out loud. "I suppose we can manage. I'll cover where I can. You tell Dianna not to worry. Go, be with her family. We'll see her next week, dear."

"You're the best, Judy. Bye." He pressed end and handed the phone back to me. "There, all done. Easy as that." John's long arms wrapped around my frame and pulled me closer. And, for a moment, I let him make me forget about everything. The next few days were going to be hard on me. I was about to do something I hadn't done since I graduated high school ten years ago.

I was going home.

***

Thanks to the stupid tourist season, the only flight available was that same day, the red-eye. As the car rolled to a stop in front of the departures entrance at the Edmonton Airport, I inhaled deeply before looking to John. "Are you sure I can't just turn back and ignore my family for the rest of my life?"

He tipped his head and gave me that look, the one that said, *grow up, Dianna*. But he could see the nerves coming to the surface and quickly softened. He reached over and cupped my face in one of his massive palms and I let the warmth of his skin calm me.

"Babe, you'll be fine. You don't owe anyone anything. Just go, help with the funeral, and sort out the stuff in the house. You'll be home before you know it."

I pulled away and gave a slight nod. I wanted him to be right. I really did. But I knew my family, and this trip was going to be the furthest thing from pleasant. When I finished high school, I was expected to stay behind and help run the family business. When I immediately left the island for college, I created quite the stir.

I was treated like an outcast. As if everyone assumed I thought I was too good to stay behind in small-town Newfoundland and settle. Then, when I finished college and still didn't return... well, let's just say I became a traitor. The people of my tiny community are a proud bunch, and once I became a mainlander, I was no longer part of it. Sure, they put on a super happy, but equally fake, smiles when they spoke to me.

But that was just for show.

"Okay," I sucked in one more deep breath, "here I go. Wish me luck."

John smiled; the kind that reaches the eyes and creates little crinkles. "You don't need it. You're overthinking it all."

I leaned in and planted a kiss on his lips and then exited the car. I grabbed my carry on from the back seat and waved to him as he pulled away from the curb. After I entered the sliding doors of the departures section, I made my way over to the WestJet counter to check in.

"Good morning!" the chipper lady with a teal neck scarf greeted. "Do you have anything to check?"

I handed her my ID with a meek smile. "Nope, just a carry on." I watched as she punched in my info on the computer.

"Oh, heading to Newfoundland, are we?"

I pretended to fiddle with something in my purse. "Yep."

"I hear it's really great this time of year. Are you going for business or pleasure?" she asked. The poor woman, she was just trying to be friendly, do her job. But, honestly, I hardly ever spoke or even thought about Newfoundland. I had wiped my hands of my roots a long time ago. It was just too hard to think of my beloved home and the painful memories that went with it.

"Neither. Death in the family." That should shut the conversation down pretty fast.

Her face paled and she tipped her head with remorse. "Oh, dear, I'm so sorry to hear." She printed off my ticket and handed it back to me with my ID. "Well, Hopefully, next time will be under better circumstances."

"*Hopefully*, there won't be a next time," I replied flatly, then headed off to security.

***

Airplanes weren't my thing. I was hastily reminded why when I was jostled from my coma-like sleep, the hard metal arm of my chair drove into my side. I attempted to blink away the cloudy film that filled my eyes, still drowsy from the high dose of Dramamine I tossed back just a couple of hours earlier. The plane's cabin was shrouded in the dim light of the midnight flight, but its occupants were alert with panic as we battled some rough turbulence. A bing from the intercom shot through the space like a sharp echo.

"This is your captain speaking. We're just approaching the coast of Newfoundland and have encountered some turbulence. Rest assured that everything will be fine once we drop out of this altitude. Bear with us as we enter a quick decline. Thank you."

My stomach scrambled to the base of my throat as the plane suddenly dropped, my ears buckling from the pressure of the elevation change. The beds of my fingernails protested as my fingertips dug into the underside of the armrests and I attempted to breathe through the chaos. But we, thankfully, leveled out and the plane soon coasted back into a steady pace. I let out a heavy breath and pried my hands from their grip, the adrenaline subsiding and dissipating in my chest.

I hated flying. Give me the sea any day.

There was no way I'd get back to sleep at that point, so I pushed up my window blind and gazed down at the vast blackness of the cold ocean below. But, within moments, the stunning rocky coast of my homeland came into view, the landscape aglow in the barely rising sun, and my heart fluttered. From this height, the scattered lights across the coast looked like little fireflies, stationary, but still beautiful nonetheless.

I watched as we descended, the details of the landscape sharpening the closer we got. My only regret was not being able to get a daytime flight, so I could appreciate the raw beauty in a better light. Still, the flood of the night sky didn't diminish anything, only created a different version of it when mixed with the glow of the coming sun. The thick green forests were dense and dark and wrapped themselves around the tiny communities of firefly lights like lazy, black snakes.

"Beautiful, isn't it?"

I nearly jumped out of my skin as a quiet shriek escaped my throat and looked to the passenger next to me. An elderly man. He grinned at me. "Sorry, dear, didn't mean to startle you."

I returned the smile. "No, it's okay," I chuckled, "I was just… daydreaming."

"Hard not to when you're faced with somethin' like that, 'eh?" He lifted his chin and motioned at my window. The old man then leaned in closer, to get a better look, and I shifted so he could. "I'll never get tired of this view. I fly out to Alberta half a dozen times a year to see the grandkids, and I love every second of it." He paused to heave a thoughtful sigh. "But there's nothing quite like the trip home."

"I would have to disagree with you there. I despise flying."

"Oh, yes, the flight is dreadful. Too long." The man looked back at the window. "But that right there is worth it. To see my home from up here. The majesty of it all. It's absolutely magical."

Oh, he was one of those people. The old-timers who still believed in the fables of my home province. We have a heavy history of British ancestors, but with a sprinkle of Irish and Scottish mixed in. My Aunt Mary was one. So was my mother. Dad hated every bit of it, so she only ever told me stories when he was absent; fairies, mermaids, and witches. I used to love it.

"Are you coming home or just visiting?"

"Um, coming home. Funeral." My gaze then dropped to my lap where my fingers fussed with the bottom button on my jacket. Being that close to home made the reality of it hit sharper. Harder. A woolly lump formed in my throat and I swallowed hard to force it down.

The old man placed his hand over one of mine on the armrest and gave it a squeeze. "Oh, m'dear, I'm so sorry for your loss." Silence filled the tiny space between us as he waited for me to reply, but I couldn't. "Someone close?"

I nodded and was startled at the sudden sensation of wetness in my eyes. I had been so strong. Aside from the initial phone call from my aunt, I never really fought with tears over my father's death and I realized what the trigger was. The old man. He reminded me too much of Dad. The Dad I knew before my mother passed away. The loving sweetness, the alertness in his eyes... before it all faded away with the agony of her death. But it seemed the old man could sense my pain.

"So, whereabouts are you from?" he asked, changing the subject.

I blinked away the teary film and slipped my hand out from under his hold to rub my eyes. "West Coast. Just outside of Deer Lake, by Gros Morne."

"Ah, pirates," he replied, "gorgeous over there. We go to Marble Mountain every Winter."

"Pirates?" I asked, confused.

He just chuckled. "You don't know your own history?"

"Well, yes, I do. Sort of. I mean, I know my Dad's side, I guess." I felt like he was about to school me. I knew, as most Newfoundlanders do, that our province had a lot of ties to piracy back in the day. "I thought the whole pirate stuff happened on the East Coast, over by St. John's? What was his name, Easton, or something?"

"Ah, so you do know?" he replied with a cheeky grin. "Yes, Peter Easton was probably our most famous pirate. But not the only one. The West Coast was riddled with them. All those coves and bays, lined with caves and whatnot to hide their treasures."

"That's cool. My mom was a historian, of sorts. More like a collector, I guess. She was obsessed with collecting and archiving everything she could get her hands on that had even the slightest thing to do with the history of the area. I'm going home now to sort through it all, actually. I'll keep an eye out for any pirate stuff."

I laughed then, but I was serious. I really would. As a kid, I remember adoring my mother's things, her precious possessions that she coveted so much. Things like scrolls and books, ancient fishing tools and really old swords. They littered our home, hanging on walls and filling glass cabinets, but the chests were my favorite. I always imagined they were pirates' chests, full of cursed treasure.

"You speak about your mother in the past tense. Is her death the unfortunate reason you're coming home?"

I chewed the inside of my cheek, my go-to nervous bad habit when I felt anxious or stressed. Over the last decade, these few words were the most I'd spoken of my mother out loud. "Um, no. She passed away when I was a teenager. It's my dad. He died yesterday."

More hand squeezing.

"I'm so sorry for all your loss. Too young. You're far too young to be left alone in this world, m'love," he said, comforting me with a term of endearment I hadn't heard in years.

"It's okay," I assured him and pointed my gaze out the window. "I'm used to it. I've been alone for a long time."

The familiar bing came across the intercom once more. "*This is your captain speaking. We've landed in Deer Lake at the Deer Lake Regional Airport at about a quarter past five. The temperature is currently eleven degrees Celsius on this warm August morning and is expected to rise to the mid-twenties by late afternoon. For those who are visiting Newfoundland for the first time, welcome, and thank you for flying with West Jet. For those who are residents of the province... welcome home.*"

I inhaled deeply. Yes, welcome home, indeed.

CHAPTER TWO

I sent John a quick *I'm here* text before I made my way through the crowd exiting the plane and headed toward the tiny area of the minuscule Deer Lake airport where I knew my aunt would be waiting for me. I worried that I wouldn't recognize her, or vice versa. It had been well over a decade after all.

But then those thoughts quickly dissipated when my eyes scanned the crowd and landed on a quirky woman with crazy grey, curly hair that was slopped atop of her head in a haphazard messy bun. Long strands fell loose around her shoulders and even touched the back of her rainbow-colored knit sweater. Her welcome smile eased my nerves and I fell, awkwardly, into her open arms. She smelled like homemade bread and an open fire.

"My girl." She grabbed me by the upper arms and pushed me away from her body. "Let me get a look at ch'ya." Aunt Mary scanned me up and down with a fierce and proud grin. "Just as I thought. Too beautiful for your own good. I see you finally figured out how to tame those damn curls.

"It's good to see you, Aunt Mary, you haven't changed a bit."

We both stood and smiled at one another until she looped her arm in mine. "Come on then, let's get you fed."

"Did you, by chance, bake bread?" I asked, my mouth filling with saliva at the thought of my favorite childhood food.

Aunt Mary would bake a batch of loaves every Sunday and I could smell it from down the gravel road we all lived on. I'd go running to her house on those days, and she'd have a special loaf, just for me, set aside. A small, one-bun, loaf and I'd take it down by the ocean side to sit on a rock and eat it. The whole dang thing.

She gave me a sideways look. "Of course. Company comin'."

I wrapped my sweater tight across my chest as we exited the airport and the moist East Coast air blanketed me. I grinned as we kept our pace across the small parking lot toward her car. "Did you, by any chance, save some of the dough?"

"Still love your toutans, do ya?" Mary chuckled. "I did. Hope you're hungry."

I was. But that wouldn't have mattered. Newfoundland hospitality meant you were going to be forced to eat more than you could handle, whether you liked it or not. Luckily for Aunt Mary, I loved it. Growing up around so much comfort food was the reason I became a chef. I would have become a baker, like my parents, but then I would have been guilted even more about moving back home.

The hour-long drive back to my childhood home was lengthy and nerve-wracking. Glorious, long-forgotten shades of the green landscape filled my vision and brought memories to the surface; both happy and sad. The closer we got, the more my brain spun with thoughts of seeing my family.

The questions, the odd looks, the shared memories of Dad that I won't understand because I hadn't been there in years. A fact that they all know and will surely use to pile on the guilt. They'll be talking about him, sharing stories, and I'll just sit there, unknowing, on the outside. Mary seemed to sense my unease and let a comfortable silence fill the car. I took a deep breath and tried to remember John's wise words.

You don't owe anyone anything.

It helped. A little. He just didn't understand the history of my life. The craziness that was my childhood; growing up with a mother who seemed to be from another world with her outrageous stories of magic and wonder, and a father who was as much a realist as the sky is blue.

They were such an odd couple but loved each other fiercely. It was a love I admired my whole life, a love I aspired to have someday. Things were getting there with John. For me, anyway. He was like a lone wolf that I tamed and brought home. And I constantly worried that he'd one day realize the door was left open.

But, yeah, my parents. Mom was like the glue that kept us together. And not just us, but the whole community. She ran that bakery and made everything with love. Kids got free cookies every Sunday, she donated freshly baked bread to less fortunate families, and she even used some old recipes that were passed down through generations in her family.

Braided bread contraptions too pretty to eat, stone-fired buns infused with rosemary. Everyone looked forward to the smells emitted from our bakery each and every day. After she died, after we lost her to the sea… things changed. Dad tried his best to keep the bakery running, but it was like Bert taking over for Ernie's job. It just wasn't the same.

Aunt Mary began to slow on the highway, so I knew we were approaching our exit to my small hometown community of Rocky Harbour. As we drove through the winding roads toward my aunt's house, I gazed out the window at the landscape that rushed by. Nothing had changed. Not a single thing. Every tree, every rock, still exactly as I remembered it. As if time stood still while I was away and my arrival kick-started a motion picture that now played out in front of me.

As we passed children riding bikes and endless lines of clothes drying in the warm summer breeze, I became more certain in my decision to not come back and settle. I wasn't built for small-town life.

Yet, I hadn't truly settled in Edmonton, either. I'd find my forever home someday, I knew, deep down, that I was on the right path. I just had to keep following it. I just wished there were a big flashing sign or something. *This is it, this is your life*!

"So," Mary finally broke the silence, "how does it feel to be home?"

I was about to plaster on a fake smile but one look at her told me not to. There was something about my great aunt, the one family member who always told it to me like it was, never missed a birthday or Christmas card, that made me comfortable around her.

"Truthfully?"

"Always," she replied sternly, gripping the steering wheel as we made a sharp turn.

"It feels weird. Like I shouldn't be here."

We then pulled into her driveway, a long gravel stretch that ended with her house and a steep drop to the ocean side.

"Dianna, m'dear. You have every right to be here as anyone. You're your father's only child, and it would be wrong for you *not* to be here. You understand me?"

I smiled and nodded.

"Now, let's get inside and get some food on the table."

"Okay," I answered. "I'll just get my bag."

Mary scuttled into the house while I grabbed my modest carry-on from the trunk. As I closed the hatch, the sweet smell of ocean whipped through my hair and across my face, leaving a light mist on my skin and I inhaled deeply. I may not belong there, but I did belong to the ocean. That much I knew for certain. As a kid, I'd run and play along this gravel road where my family lived. Aunts, uncles, cousins, and us. But most of my time was spent by myself, down by the water, gazing out to the horizon and building rafts to try and get there.

"Dianna! You comin'?" Aunt Mary called from the front porch, yanking me out of my daydream.

"Yeah, I'll be right there."

My chest heaved as I ached to leave the gorgeous view that stretched out as far as the eye could see. There was nothing after this. The closest piece of land was Quebec, across the St. Lawrence. To me, there was something comforting in an endless horizon. Go where you want, as far as you can, with nothing to stop you. Unlike life on land, where there's something to face every which way you turned.

***

After the heaviest breakfast ever; a pile of fried bread dough drowned in syrup, I sat on her back porch with a cup of tea in hand. I smiled at the delicate piece of china, a dainty thing with hand-painted roses and a gold rim. I pulled out my phone to check if John had replied to my text but was disappointed to see he hadn't. Mary was inside, fussing around the kitchen, clanking pots and pans as she cleaned up. Soon, she emerged and sidled up next me in her rocking chair.

"How you feelin', dear? Tired? You want to go lay down for a bit? I got the spare room all done up for ya."

I shook my head. "No, thanks. As much as I'd love to fall into a coma after that meal, I should probably get some work done. The funeral's tomorrow, right? What time?"

She reached over and pat my arm. "Now, don't you go worryin' about that stuff. I took care of it all. Your father made me swear. He had everything planned out, right down to the very last detail."

I laughed. "Yeah, sounds like Dad. Such a stickler."

"The funeral is at eleven, then everyone's comin' back here for lunch." She gently rocked her chair and sipped her tea.

"Oh? Do you need help to make food, then?" Surely, if I knew my aunt at all, there wouldn't be a deli tray in sight. All homemade, no doubt.

She grinned and gave me a wink. "Nope. Had everything pre-made and in the deep freeze since yesterday morning. Plus, I imagine people will bring stuff."

"Well, now I feel useless."

Her face turned serious as her rocking came to a halt and she leaned forward. "I don't think you understand the state over at your father's house, Dianna. In his last few months, he went mad going through your mother's things, lookin' for… something. I dunno." She shook her head and took another sip of tea. "You'll be busy over there, for sure."

Perfect. I needed something to keep me distracted from thoughts of the funeral. Plus, it was a great way to avoid seeing the rest of my distant family. I stood up and downed the last of my tea which was mostly milk and sugar at that point.

"Do you have a key? I can head over there now. I only have so much time here, better make use of it, I guess."

She gave me a sympathetic look before standing from her own chair. "Come on, then. I'll bring you over."

The drive was short, just a few minutes down to the opposite end of the gravel road. It was just how I remembered it; bumpy and narrow. But I was shocked to see the state of my childhood home as it slowly came into view, like seeing a grandparent for the first time in ten years and trying to hide your devastation over their drastic aging.

The house was once a beautiful two-story, with a giant turret that provided a wicked view of the ocean. On the first level, the turret housed part of my mom's office. On the second story, it was my old bedroom and I loved it dearly. Mom had insisted on it being my room, said it was where I was meant to be.

Never really understood what she meant, but now... I think I did. I spent endless hours sitting by the window, staring out onto the ocean water, watching the hypnotic waves and letting the crystal reflection of the sun on its surface burn my eyes. And then, at night, I'd watch obsessively as the moon played with the waves lapping in its light.

But now, I was faced with an aging property, one that had clearly been neglected. The old-fashioned wood siding, once a cape cod blue, had faded into a lifeless grey. Pieces had fallen off and sat on the ground below, the relentless grass grew over parts of the boards which gave me an idea of how long they had been lying there. Some windows in the second story had been boarded up. I wondered then, what had my father's state of mind really been like these last few years and my chest filled with anxious waves of guilt and regret.

Was it my fault?

I followed Aunt Mary to the front step, careful to avoid the bottom one that was clearly rotting, the rust-colored wood peeking out through cracks and missing chunks. I hopped up to the third step and then made my way across the large front porch as she unlocked the door.

It opened with a loud creak, threatening to fall off its hinges and, as I stepped over the threshold, the familiar scent of my childhood punched me in the face. The distinct smell of old books, a wood-burning fire, and leather. It never lessened, even after all these years. The only thing missing was the pleasant taint of baked goods, which aired out with my mother's passing years ago.

I looked at Mary. "What the heck happened? Why did Dad let the house get this way?"

She shrugged apologetically. "Who knows, m'love? The mind of a dying man is a lonely place."

She walked over to the woodstove and tossed in a small log along with some crumbled-up sales flyers from the box next to it. Within a minute she'd had a fire going and closed the cast iron door.

"He left it to you, though. That much I know."

My heart fluttered. "The house?"

"Yep, like I said before, and the bakery. Along with a bunch of other stuff. It's all in the will. We can go over it tonight when you're done here if you want."

All these years, especially after my dad got sick, I always said to myself that I didn't want any of it. No reason to come back. But now, being here, seeing the state of what's left of my past life... I felt an odd compulsion to stake a claim. To fix it. Make it mine. It's what my mom would want.

"That would be nice, thanks." I glanced around at the fairly empty front room. "So, where should I start?"

Mary rolled her eyes. "Follow me."

She brought me down the hallway toward the end of the house that faced the ocean. But the blaring sunlight that I remembered once filling the space and pouring out from my mother's office was missing. Instead, I walked down a shadowed hall half-filled with aging boxes, papers spilling out of them and onto the floor below my feet. When I came to the mouth of the room, I nearly choked on my breath.

Mom's office. It was a disaster. The hallway was like a preview of what was contained in the circular space. Towers of boxes, half falling apart, papers flooding the floor, unable to even see the beautiful hardwood I knew lay beneath it. Her antique desk, once a giant in the room, was now dwarfed by the mountain of stuff that smothered its surface.

Mary looked at me and slapped her arms at her sides. "I imagine this is as good a place as any to start. There's a lot of things of your mother's that the museum wants. But it's up to you what goes and what stays." She turned and headed toward the door, patting me on the shoulder first and then handing me the key. "I'll leave you to it. Call over to the house if you need anything."

***

Five hours later, I'd barely made a dent. All I managed to do was create more of a mess, it seemed. But I had attempted to organize things, at least. Four piles laid out on the floor in front of me, each marked by a box.

One for papers that seemed to be important to our direct family, one for certificates of authentication so I could match them to objects later, one of straight-up garbage, and then the miscellaneous pile. The biggest one. The further I went, the more I worried about my father's state of mind before he passed away.

Why was he looking through boxes of scrolls and books that held birth certificates dated as far back as the early 1600s? I even found one box in the hallway that was literally just full of broken things; buttons, ripped pictures, jewelry, dishes. Most of the items were Mom's, which I found really odd. Was he taking out some frustrations? Was it evidence that he attempted to clean up Mom's stuff? Or perhaps the box was just that; a container of broken things my mother couldn't part with. I'll never know.

I tossed another random piece of paper in the garbage pile and looked out the big bay window of Mom's office. I may have created more of a mess, but I did bring the height of it all down. The gorgeous view the space once offered now re-emerged and the orange-blue sunset cast an eerie and magical glow across the room.

My mind wandered through the library of memories it held as I starred out upon the ocean water, watching the way the twilight waves came to life in the moonlight and played with the colorful reflection of the setting sun. The only time of day the two worlds met. I remembered then, something my mom once told me.

"You see that, sweetie?" she'd asked, pointing out to the water as I stood on the deep window bench in my room. "The moon and the sun playing together. Isn't it beautiful?"

I nodded, in awe of the gorgeous display but also my mother's soothing voice. Soft as sugar and milk on bread. She bent down then and spoke quietly in my ear.

"It's the only time the two can meet. The sun and the moon, touching like that. It's magic, Dianna. Don't forget that."

"What kind of magic?" I asked.

"If you were to sail out there, to the water, and meet the moon and the sun in the waves at just the right time, they'd grant you a wish."

"Just one?"

"If you knew what you wanted, one is all you'd need, baby." She caressed my cheek and tucked a knot of dark curls behind my little ear.

I smiled at my mother and looked back out toward the water, so certain, even at that delicate age, of what I wanted. "I'd wish to sail away on an adventure and fall in love with a prince!"

Mom laughed and kissed my cheek. "Always remember that you don't need a prince to have the adventure of your dreams, Dianna, baby."

"I know, Mommy." I grinned up at her. "But it would be more fun with someone to share it with."

My eyes filled with tears at the memory. God, I loved my mother. She was unlike anyone I've ever known. She loved relentlessly, was never angry, and dreamed of things no one could ever fathom. I used to be just like her. It's funny, really, removed for so long from my father's realist personality and infinite sadness... I somehow managed to become just like him.

I decided to take a break.

After checking my phone to see if John had replied yet and frowning when I saw he still hadn't, I wandered out to the kitchen, hoping there was something in the fridge and lucked out with a bottle of water and an apple fruit cup. I wondered what he was doing. I'd been gone for nearly a day and he never replied or called me yet. The three-and-a-half-hour time change was a pain, yes, but still. I quickly punched in a short text to say hi and remind him to call me.

I wandered the house, slurping back the pureed apples and taking note of all the things I still had to go through. Approaching the base of the large, dark staircase, I ascended upstairs to see what awaited me. My parent's room was surprisingly decent. It seemed that Dad kept things the way I remembered, only a couple of small boxes sat next to his side of the bed. The image made me frown as the thought of him still sleeping on his side, after all these years, popped in my head.

I moved on to my childhood bedroom and peeked my head inside. My heart sank when I found nothing but a glorified storage locker. Boxes, trunks, totes, and bags filled the space. I stepped inside and opened the flaps of one of the cardboard cartons marked with my name and smiled.

To anyone else, it would have appeared to be a collection of random things tossed inside, but I knew the items. My parents took me to St. John's one year, I was no more than eight or nine years old. We always took a trip each Summer, after tourist season died down and right before school started. That year, we went to Signal Hill. It rained so hard. I was so bummed that we couldn't do any of the hiking trails, so Mom and Dad took me to a gift shop and bought just about everything in it.

I smiled at the memory as I pulled out a key chain; a tiny snow globe hung from it with a model of Signal Hill inside. I fished the house key from my pocket and attached it to the trinket before stuffing it back in my jeans.

I finished my fruit cup and tossed the empty container in the bathroom trashcan before heading back downstairs. As I descended, I could feel a chill in the air, as prominent as the silence which filled the rooms, so I made my way over to the woodstove and stoked the near-dead fire. The coals were still piping hot, and the glowy red came back to life as I poked it with the metal rod. I grabbed another log and tossed it in. While I waited for the flame to take it, something caught my eye. A lone box, sitting on the dining room table just a few feet away.

I closed the heavy iron door of the woodstove and latched the handle before making my way over to the table and realized the box was, in fact, a small trunk, one of those of my mother's that I adored in my childhood. Pure moonlight filled the space, the orange blaze of the sleepy sun now gone, replaced by the cool white glow of the massive August moon blaring in through the picture window next to the table.

The trunk, an old leather-covered box about the size of a small carry-on suitcase, didn't jog my memory at all. I wondered where Mom had this one poked away. And, why was it there, all alone, on my Dad's dining room table?

My fingers ran over the rough surface, taking note of the once dark red leather and how it had weathered into a murky brown over who knows how many decades. Along the edges, near the seams, I could see hints of the deep, rust color it once sported. Hand-forged brass tacks decorated the edges and matched the heavy lock at the center.

The trunk was small, but beautiful, and should be easy enough to take back on the plane. I decided, then, that I would fill it with the things I wanted to keep for myself and leave the other piles for my aunt to distribute as I saw fit. But my idea stopped short when I realized the lock was, in fact, locked and there was no key in sight.

"Great," I said with an exhausted sigh and glanced around the room. All the built-in shelves, nooks and crannies, where the heck would I find something as small as a key? And one specifically for that chest? My mother had hundreds of old keys lying around; some for her many chests and cabinets, some decorative, and others she was too scared to throw away in case they belonged to something she'd need in the future. "Come on, Dad. You had this one out for a reason. Where did you put the key?"

I began to wander, feeling around on high shelves, running my hands along the tops of cabinets. I found a load of dust bunnies, a few crumpled up receipts, and three paper clips. But no key. Then I remembered a tin of them I'd found earlier, in Mom's office, and ran to grab it. It was heavy for its small size and plunked down on the marble-topped table with a clank that resounded through the dead silent space.

"Okay, first thing's first," I pulled out my phone to put on some music and saw that I had a notification. John had finally replied to my text.

Are you coming?

What was he talking about? My flight wasn't until Sunday night, but my thumbs punched in the letters of a reply.

Miss me already?

A speedy response popped back.

I always miss you, baby.

My heart fluttered. It may have taken a long time, but John was finally settling, and he was doing it with me. My grin stretched from ear to ear as I began typing back a lengthy reply, telling him about my day and how much I missed him, too. But before I could finish, he texted me again.

So, are you coming over or what? Dianna doesn't get back until Sunday.

My fingers turned to jelly, and the phone fell to the floor. At the same time, that familiar anvil dropped in my stomach with a heavy *thump* and I nearly puked all over the table in front of me. The silence of the room rang heavy in my ears and heat filled my face as my heart began to race. My hand grabbed the edge of the table, knees suddenly weak.

That bastard.

I took a few deep breaths before retrieving my phone from the floor and began typing a reply, my thumbs flying across the tiny keys. Fury and rage, fueled by betrayal, coursed through my body but my mind rang through for a brief second to tell me one important thing.

Find out who he's cheating on me with.

I deleted the message I'd typed so far and punched in a few new letters before hitting send.

I'll come over if you say my name.

I waited, my body on overdrive as the adrenaline pushed blood through it. Was that dumb? Had he realized he's been messaging me and not some other woman?

I'll say it now and I'll say it again, later, after you scream mine, Emily, baby.

My co-worker? That scum! My fingers trembled as I struggled to type back a final reply.

Better double-check that, asshole. You're right, I'll be home on Sunday, and you better be long gone.

I threw my phone down on the table, not caring if the screen broke, and wandered the house once more, stomping as I went about aimlessly. My life got completely turned inside out this week. My father died, I'd inherited a property along with a slew of garbage, and now the man I thought I loved was cheating on me with the nineteen-year-old hostess at work.

I made my way back around to the dining room to let out a fierce, guttural scream as I picked up and heaved the small trunk at the wall. It was the loudest sound I'd heard all day and it fell to the floor where it busted open, its contents spilling out around it.

I needed a drink.

CHAPTER THREE

After rummaging around in Dad's liquor cabinet of near-empty flasks, I finally found a half-full bottle of Newfoundland Screech and hastily put the mouth to my lips. I chugged down a huge gulp and then let out a gargle as it scorched my throat.

"Who needs a freakin' glass?" I tipped back another swig of the rum, glancing down at the mess I'd made, waiting for the liquor to drown my anger.

I sauntered over to the heap of contents that had spilled from the small trunk and sat down, crisscrossing my legs and nestling the bottle of rum in the nook they created. First, I picked up the overturned trunk, noting that the lock hadn't been broken, just popped open, and I set it aside.

A pile of dirty red fabric caught my eye next. I pulled it toward me, stretching it out and assessing just what it was. A jacket. A really old jacket. But, unlike other ancient garments I recall my mother archived, this one didn't feel so delicate. I remembered once, she'd been preparing an old white blouse for display at the museum, I reached up to touch it and it felt like tissue in between my fingers.

This peacoat style jacket was thick, like leather but not. Heavy gold buttons and clasps lined the center from top to bottom, a wide collar crowned the top, and the blood-red color of the fabric was still prominent aside from the visible wear and tear. It brought to mind a captain's jacket, part of the old uniforms characters wore in movies and on TV, with the funny white trousers and shoes with big buckles on the front.

I loved it. The jacket was definitely coming back to Alberta with me. I gently folded it and set it aside with the trunk and moved on to the other items sprawled on the floor in front of me. A massive compass made of brass, it covered my entire palm and appeared to still work, despite the cracked glass face. A thick, brown leather scabbard that held a large dagger. I unsheathed the old knife, surprised at its sharpness. The handle was made of light-colored wood, clearly hand carved or something, with the initials M.L.C. etched into the hilt.

"Cool," I spoke to myself as I sheathed it and set it aside in the growing pile next to me.

Next, a journal. Thick and well-loved, the book was bound in black leather with the spine held together in a stiff sort of twine. The initials H.W. was burned on the cover and I wondered why the initials would be different than that of the ones I'd found on the dagger's handle. I stopped for a moment and looked at the contents as a whole, noting the few silver coins that also sat on the floor, and realized just what this trunk was.

"This is a pirate's chest." A grin smeared across my face. "A real freakin' pirate's chest."

As a child, I always imagined that the cool things my mother brought home once belonged to pirates and other shady individuals. But, as an adult, I looked back on those memories and told myself I was being silly. Now, though... this was proof that I was right. John would flip if he saw this. I told him all about my childhood obsession and...

"Damn it." The sting of his betrayal poured over my wounds again, I'd forgotten about him for a brief moment, distracted by my awesome discovery. I grabbed the bottle of rum from between my legs and downed a few more mouthfuls. How could I have so easily forgotten the jerk? I still couldn't believe he had cheated on me. Was probably cheating on me at that very moment, in fact.

But a part of me, a very small part, wasn't really that surprised. I should have known, and I felt like a complete idiot then, as I replayed our relationship in my mind. I was always the one to initiate things.

A second date, the first kiss, meeting his parents, moving in together. They were all my ideas, and I remembered some of them taking more convincing than they should have. John was a flirter, a schmoozer, a lady's man. I was a fool to think I could tame him, make him settle. I just wanted it so bad. To share my life with someone, to share my adventure.

I drank some more.

The abrupt sound of knocking at the door pulled me down from my mountain of sorrow for a moment. The nearly empty bottle tucked neatly under my arm as I made my way toward the front door, with a slight wobble in my step. The old brass deadbolt gave me grief as I fiddled with it, but the door finally opened to reveal my aunt.

"Oh, so you *are* alive," she said, eyeballing the bottle of rum under my arm as I leaned my entire weight against the door frame. In her hands was a large glass dish covered in tin foil and the warm smell of home-cooked food wafted up across my nose. "Looks like you need this more than I thought."

I let her in and began to walk back toward the dining room, swigging back more rum. The liquid sat heavy in my stomach and warmed my veins. I glanced at the clock and saw that I'd been there at the house for nearly eight hours. My aunt's sudden arrival reminded me that, aside from the fruit cup, I'd been drinking on an empty stomach.

"I brought some leftover lasagna I made for supper, thinking you'd be back to the house. I bet you're starving." She cleared some space on the table and grabbed a couple of plates from the kitchen. "How're things going here, anyway? Makin' a dent?"

I laughed and took another mouthful from the bottle. "I have no clue what I'm doing. There's so much crap in that room. I should just throw it all in the trash and go back home." Another swig. "Oh, wait. I can't go back home. My boyfriend is cheating on me and if I see him, I may very well beat him to death." I scooped up my fork and lobbed off a huge chunk of lasagna straight from the dish and shoved it in my mouth. "Better off staying here in my mountain of garbage," I added, motioning around the house with my fork, pieces of food falling out of my mouth.

Aunt Mary just nodded, letting me vent, I didn't even argue when she carefully slipped the bottle out of my hand. "I didn't know you had a man," she said, sitting down to eat her piece of pasta. She eyeballed the side of the dish I'd been digging into. "Keep eatin'."

I shoveled in a few more bites and chewed with one side of my mouth. "Correction. I did have a man. I told him to vamoose before I get home on Sunday." My stomach protested at the sudden influx of food I'd been heaping into it, so I put the fork down. "Although, at the rate I'm going, I may never leave this house."

Mary reached across the table, placed her hand over mine and gave it a little squeeze. "Dianna, I can help, you know? With everything. I didn't want to dig too far, I didn't..." she let go and leaned back in her chair, "I just didn't know what you wanted to keep. What was special to you. It's been so long."

I couldn't look her in the face. Staying away for so long was just as much my fault as it was Dad's. He pushed me away, but I never pushed back. I wanted to go. Living in the pit of despair my father dug for himself after my mother's passing was torture for me. He shut me out, became depressed, completely ignored my needs as a child. Yeah, I was a teen, but I still needed my daddy. The only person I had that showed me love and compassion and cared enough to check-in was... Mary.

I tore my gaze away from the dark patio window then and looked at my great aunt. This wonderful woman who loved my mother dearly, kept my dad alive when he was sick, helped run my family's business when no one could... who nurtured my broken heart so many years ago. Staying away from Dad was understandable. Staying away from Mary was wrong. I hadn't even realized until then.

"I'm so sorry, Aunt Mary. You're right. It's been way too long. I'm freaking horrible." My eyes began to pool with tears and I wiped one away as it tried to escape. "I promise to come back and visit more, okay?" I let out a bubbly sigh and crossed my arms, leaning back in my chair. My stomach was doing strange things and I fought back a belch. "Especially now that I have the house."

She perked up, a smile spreading far a wide. "You mean, you're not going to sell it?"

I shrugged. "Why would I sell it?" Another vomity belch attempted to make its way up my throat. "Maybe the bakery. I mean, I can't run it from Alberta."

"You could always move back home. Fix up the house. Run the bakery." Mary made it seem as if this were a new idea, but something told me she'd been mulling it over for a long time. She spoke with such confidence and practice. She looked at me then, eyes glistening with hope.

"Mary…" I heaved a sigh. I hated letting her down. "I can't–I have a life in Alberta. A job I've worked hard to get. You have no idea."

"So, what?"

Her curt reply caught me off guard, I hardly knew how to respond.

"You said yourself, your man is no good. If you've done nothing but focus on your career, then I 'magine you don't got many friends up there." She wasn't wrong about that. "Think about it. You could go from working for someone else to owning your own business. You can use your God-given talent every day."

Her words stewed in my brain as I chewed my lip. It was hard to formulate an argument because everything Mary said made total sense. I'd be crazy not to do it. I'd been given a tremendous opportunity. A house, a business, family to reconnect with, a community to call my own. I missed Newfoundland. We all did. Those of us who leave... we all yearn to come back. Its raw beauty, the culture. Like some sort of ancient magic calls to us. Begging our return to the sea.

I stood then. "I can't."

Mary turned to follow me with her stare. "But-"

Suddenly, I ran to the half bath off the kitchen and threw myself down, barely making it to the toilet. Rum and lasagna filled the bowl and left my body convulsing until there was nothing left. My throat burned, raw from vomit and the not-hardly-chewed food that scrapped across it, but Mary stood behind me and pulled back my hair, patting and rubbing my back.

"My poor girl," she spoke, "this brings back memories of your teens." Mary laughed, the sound deep and raspy. "You'd go out drinking to those shed parties and come crawling in through my door at all hours of the night. Too scared to go home and face your father."

I turned my head and rested my cheek against the cold toilet seat. "Not scared of him. I was scared of myself. Of what I'd say to him." I began to cry again, hot tears filled my eyes, overflowed and coursed down across my face. "I didn't want to add to his misery. He was so sad... so lost."

"I know, m'love, I know." Mary held my hair in her hands and brushed it with her fingers, gently forming it into a ponytail. "You always had this gorgeous nest of black curls. Just like your mom. Everyone always admired her beauty. Soft, tanned skin. Even in the winter. You're the spit right outta her mouth, Dianna."

I cried some more, unable to control the heaving sobs that erupted from my gut. "I miss her so much." My eyes demanded to close, and my head spun. But I could feel the soft brush of tissue against my skin as Mary wiped the tears, snot, and remnants of vomit from my face. "Why did it have to take her from me?"

"What, sweetie?"

"Mmm sea." I could feel myself drifting, threatening to pass out right there on the bathroom floor. The long plane ride, the emotional exhaustion, and the gut full of rum had brought me to my limit. My words slurred as I tried hard to stay awake and speak them out loud. "The sea took her away from me."

That was all I remembered. Although, I vaguely recalled Aunt Mary laying me down on the cool, white tile floor. As she propped my head up with a pillow, she muttered the words *had to* and *home*, but I couldn't piece together the sentence. I was too far gone, and I never wanted to come back.

CHAPTER FOUR

The steady flow of gravel beneath the tires created a constant hum that swirled in my vulnerable stomach and the cold glass of the window felt good on my sweaty face as I leaned against it. In the driver's seat, Aunt Mary was silent, a protest to my behavior at the funeral, I imagine.

"I'm sorry," I choked, my throat still raw from the coarse vomiting I had done the previous night. My gross, dry lips stuck together as the words crawled out.

Without even glancing at me, Mary threw up her hand. "Don't. I don't want to hear it."

The car rolled to a stop just outside my parent's house–my house–and relief flooded my body at the thought of being alone again. The funeral was pure torture for me. Surrounded by family members I'd barely recognized, all eyes on me, and the closed oak colored casket that sat like an elephant in the room.

So, naturally, I retreated into a shell the whole time and, when it was my turn to get up and speak the words purged from my body just like the rum and lasagna the night before. I couldn't help it or stop it, the words demanded to come out. All the feelings I'd bottled up over the last decade, my conflictions over my father's death, how he'd ruined my mother's legacy by letting his life and the things they'd built together just fade away and be replaced with misery.

I crossed my arms like a child and continued to stare out the window, refusing to get out until she accepted my apology. "Well, I am, though."

Mary heaved a sigh as she leaned back and let the silence hang between us. After a minute or two she finally spoke. "I know you are, Dianna." She took off her seatbelt. "I'm just disappointed, is all." Mary opened her door to get out and I reluctantly followed suit. Every movement hurt my body and threatened my stomach, but the fresh air felt good in my lungs. Mary circled the car then, coming toward me.

"You don't have to stay," I told her. "I know you have the luncheon thing at the house."

"What kind of person would I be if I just dropped you off at the curb like a bag of garbage?"

"A better person than me, probably." Hangover shivers shook through my body as I wrapped my arms tightly across my torso. "I'm just gonna go back to sleep for a few hours. I'll be fine."

Aunt Mary grabbed me by the upper arms, forcing me to look down into her face. A mess of grey curls whipped around her, as if part of the wind, and she smiled. "I know you'll be fine, Dianna. But I want you to be more than just *fine*. I'd hoped this trip home would be some sort of closure for you, that you'd be... I don't know. Happier?"

I felt compelled to tell her what she wanted to hear but couldn't bear lying to my aunt. "I know." My cold hand clasped around her warm one that still firmly held one of my shoulders. "But, for now, fine is all I can do."

She hugged me then, a quick warm embrace, and then headed back to the car. "I'll be back after everyone is gone. And I'll bring you some food."

"Sure, sounds good. Bring some for both of us. We'll eat supper together."

Mary smiled and waved before getting in her car and then I watched as she drove off down the gravel road, finally leaving me alone. Ever since the moment she peeled me off the bathroom floor that morning, all I'd wanted was to retreat to my house and sleep for a million years. I rarely drank alcohol past the point of a social drink or a glass of wine with supper. So, a hangover as heavy as the one I was experiencing felt like the closest thing to death I could imagine.

Although the ocean breeze wasn't really cold, I still shivered as I slowly made my way up the old rotting front steps. Inside, the warmth of the woodstove hugged me, and my body begged to be put to bed. I stoked the fire and tossed in another log before making my way over to the couch. The thought of climbing the stairs to a bed made me want to cry so I collapsed on the old, caramel-colored leather sofa. A heavy knitted blanket fell from the back and I stretched it out over my tired body, happy to stay there forever.

***

I awoke sometime later and I moaned in agony as my consciousness clawed its way to the surface. The heat from the woodstove, just a few feet away, in combination with my hangover from Hell, had left me extremely dehydrated. I attempted to swallow, but my mouth was completely void of any moisture. I needed water. I just didn't want to move.

I forced my arm to move and peel the woolen blanket from my aching body. The air outside of my cocoon was cool in comparison to what was held beneath it and I shivered again as I zombie-walked to the kitchen across the room. I grabbed one of the bottles of water from the fridge and downed it in seconds, my stomach threatening to protest at the sudden influx of wet and cold.

But I was fine. It settled, and I drank half of another bottle. My eyes then darted to the big clock on the wall, a mock ship's wheel with the workings of a timepiece in the center, one of Mom's favorite pieces in the house, and noted that I'd only slept for two hours. Strangely, it felt like enough. My body wanted to stay awake then, so I strolled over to my pirate's chest on the dining room table.

Immediately, I grabbed the cool red jacket, noting its convenient size, and slipped it on. It fit like a glove and smelled musty from its few lifetimes of storage. *It deserved to breathe again*, I thought as I ran my hand down one of the sleeves and smiled. "Don't you worry, one trip to the dry cleaners and you'll be my new favorite jacket." I slipped my hands into the big side pockets, surprised to find a strange object and pulled it out.

"Oh, no way."

It was a small ship-in-a-bottle. I always marveled at the intricacy, the tiny details and impossibility of them. As I brought the bottle closer to my face for a better look, I could see that this one was far more detailed than any I'd ever seen before. Through the dirty glass, I could tell that the ship wasn't the usual ones you find, with the many white sails and long, narrow boat.

No, this was most definitely a pirate's ship. The blackened wood of which it was constructed, the large stern with red windows hung on the back like a giant belly, and the three masts each displaying a weathered sheet were solid proof. The center sail sported burn holes and the faint markings of a skull.

Then something caught my eye. The fake water which held the ship in place seemed to... move. Maybe I was still waking up, and perhaps it was a trick of the light shining in through the large dining-room window.

I blinked and gave my eyes a rub with my fingers, but it didn't help. The strange resin shined like aqua jewels in the setting sun and the waves appeared to crash against the sides of the ship. Then, a red glow came from the windows of the stern. I slowly put it down on the table and noticed my bottle of rum just inches away from my hand. A sane person would look away. A sane person's stomach would roll at the very sight of it. But, clearly, from what I just witnessed... I was far from sane.

I grabbed it by the neck and downed a huge gulp, surprised that there was still some even left after last night. The liquor burned my stomach but never threatened to come back up. Choosing to ignore the ship-in-a-bottle, I glanced in my tiny trunk, pulled out the old diary I'd found yesterday and made my way over to the bay window bench seat in my mother's office.

I took another quick swig before I sat down and then tucked the bottle under my arm. My thumb ran over the burned initials once more.

"H.W. Let's find out who you were and why you have a haunted ship-in-a-bottle, shall we?"

I unraveled the old twine that held it closed and opened the black leather cover, surprised by its softness and willingness to bend. The first page read, *Henry William White*, in a beautiful inked script. A water stain had soaked into the paper and smudged the name down across the page, but it was still there, visible. "Well, I guess we know what the initials stand for." I continued on, turning the next delicate page.

June 2nd, 1698

Today is my sixteenth birthday. I have awaited this day for many years. I awoke this morning to find Mother in the kitchen, she gave me this beautiful handmade journal and began making my favorite breakfast. Fried bread and eggs covered in molasses. But I could hardly sit long enough to enjoy it. Today, Father promised I would get my own boat and I yearned to touch the sea on my own.

I ran down to the shore where I knew he would surely be, and found him standing and awaiting my arrival. He smiled and hugged me, then whispered I love you. Now that I am a man, there is no need for affirmations out loud and I was glad he thought so, as well.

He then pointed to a small boat on the water, just a few yards out. It was tiny, just large enough for myself and my gear, a single sail cast to the sky. It was magnificent. And it was mine. I spent all day out on the water. I had not dropped a single net, nor a line. I simply laid back and watched the sky as it floated above like a mirror image of my beloved sea below me.

I stopped. This was the journal of a young boy. How did it end up in a pirate's chest? Now I wondered if I had it wrong. Perhaps the trunk wasn't what I thought it was. Maybe it was just a random box that my mother collected things in. I found myself disappointed, but continue to read on.

June 10th, 1698

If my mother would allow, surely, I would live on the sea. I awake each day with vigor, eager to meet my small ship and sail the sea. If I did not bring back a basket of fish each day, I am certain Mother would have something to say. She misses me around the house and the farm, that much I know. So, I promised her I would stay home today and help her. Perhaps I shall sneak out after supper and go for a quiet moonlight sail.

The next few pages were blank, aside from the random rust-colored stains that stuck some of them together. Whatever was spilled so many centuries ago, it soaked through the paper and was left that way. I tried to pry some of the pages apart, to see if there were words trapped within, but there was nothing. Then I realized... the stains. It was blood.

I fast-forwarded through the journal, past the blots of blood to find the next journal entry. If there were any at all. Finally, I found the messy ink scratches of an entry. The same writing as Henry's but sloppier, quicker. As if they were written in haste or without care. I then noted the date. Just the very next day after the last entry.

June 11th, 1698

I should not have left. I should have listened to Mother. She caught me leaving the house after supper when the sun had set, and the moon shone over the waves just down from our farm. She told me it was dangerous, and I did not heed her warning. I told her I would only sail out a few yards. I promised.

But fate had different plans for me. For I had not even reached my boat before I met two strangers on the beach. I thought they may have been from our neighboring farm, but I was sadly mistaken.

They were pirates.

The man was silent as the female approached me, her sword drawn and hanging by her side. When I realized what they were, I begged for my life. Told them I had nothing for them to take. But the woman, Maria is what her male companion called her, forced me to lead them back to my home.

I did as I was told, frozen by fear. I assumed they would raid my home and rob my family, then retreat to their ship and sail away. I had not imagined how everything would end that night, how my life would be taken away from me.

She made me watch as she sliced my parent's throats, her male partner holding me in place. I had wet myself numerous times and vomited at his feet, but he did not sway. It felt like an eternity as I stood there, unable to move or leave or even touch my parents who lay at my feet in a pool of their own blood as Maria raided my home. She filled a gunny sack and tossed it over her shoulder before ordering her partner, Eric, to bring me along. He protested, but she insisted. His grip loosened on my arms enough for me to break away and fall at my parent's bodies, to touch them once more before the pirates carried me away. I wrapped myself around my mother's torso and cried like a small child as Eric pulled at my feet.

I don't know whether to be grateful at the sparing of my life or wish for death as I sit here on their ship, locked in a room. This journal, soaked in the blood of my mother, is the only thing I possess from my old life, only by the simple coincidence that I had it tucked into my jacket pocket.

I was surprised by the warm stream of tears that ran down my cheeks. I hadn't expected that at all. I closed the journal but then reopened it to assess the hardened brown pages with a new pair of eyes. This was Henry's journal, and the pages held the blood of his mom. What a bittersweet token to have kept. I was certain, then, that the chest was definitely that of a pirate.

I skipped ahead to try and find out whatever happened of young Henry.

July 17th, 1698

My days here on the Burning Ghost have been a series of unfortunate events. Each day brings with it a new form of torture. Eric wants nothing to do with me, for that I am thankful. But his wife, Maria, the heathen, thinks of me as a plaything. She drags me along on raids, forces me to watch while she relentlessly takes lives, leaving a trail of blood and ash in the waters.

I have become numb to the sights I behold. No longer affected by the unspeakable acts that play out before me. But that displeases Maria. She wishes me to be disgusted, to be damaged. She delights in the tears that I shed.

This evening marks the seventh time she has released me from her quarters, after forcing me into her bed. She has taken everything from me. My mother and father, my home, my life.

And now my innocence.

But that all shall end tonight. The words I now write shall be my last, and Maria will lose her toy. Ending this never-ending train of torture.

Finally, I shall be reunited with my family.

The sound of the front door creaking open pierced through the quiet house and I quickly tied the twine around Henry's journal before making my way back out to the living area. Aunt Mary was there, trays of food in hand and a smile on her face. It quickly faded, though, when she saw that I'd been crying.

She slid the heavy trays on the kitchen island top and came over to me. "What's the matter, m'love?" Mary then saw the jacket I sported. "And, w-what on Earth are you wearing?"

"Oh… a pirate's jacket?" I replied and pulled Henry's journal out from under my arm. "And I was just reading this book. It's some kind of journal from a boy who was kidnapped by pirates. They killed his parents. One was even a female. Maria or something."

Aunt Mary grabbed the trays of food from the kitchen island, brought them over to the table and sat down. She then nodded. "Ah, yes, Maria Cobham," she told me.

I was taken back at the name. "Wait, you mean -"

"Oh, yes, Dianna dear." She began scooping random bits of food onto a plate and handed it to me. "Didn't you know? Where your mother's obsession came from?"

"Maria *Cobham*?" I said, so I could hear her name in full again. "I come from pirates?" My stomach turned and rolled at the thought of my own blood committing such an unbelievable act of violence like what was done to Henry's parents.

Mary chewed a mouthful of mustard salad and then wiped her mouth with one of the flowery napkins she brought over. "Oh, yes. When your own parents met, so many years ago, your mom was fascinated with anything historic or old, she worked with the museum during the summer. It wasn't long after she met your dad that she discovered her lineage back to piracy. Then her obsession began. Of course, your father wanted nothing to do with it, he knew the awful history that came with having pirate ancestors and never wanted to be associated with it. But he adored your mom, so he let her do as she pleased," Mary waved her hand around, "like filling this house with all of her treasures."

With the tip of my fork, I picked at a small scoop of beet salad on my plate, unable to bring myself to eat it. My stomach was sick, and my heart ached for poor Henry. "So, whatever happened to the Cobhams? Maria and Eric?"

Mary shrugged. "No one really knows. They raided the Atlantic Ocean and the Gulf of St. Lawrence for years. Maria was a force to be reckoned with." She leaned in to whisper as if someone could hear us. "The stories say she was a little off, if you know what I mean?"

"Yeah, I believe it. According to this journal, she was a cold-blooded murderer and a rapist pedophile."

"Oh, no, dear. It goes far beyond that. Maria was known to torture her captives for days before tying them up in gunny sacks and tossing them overboard. *Alive*."

"Jesus..."

"She dragged her poor husband across the seas, too. Eric. Once, he turned himself in, claimed she made him do all those horrible things aboard The Burning Ghost. But Maria just came and took him, like he was her prisoner." Mary then eyed my untouched plate. "Eat."

"What's The Burning Ghost?" I asked and finally scooped some beet salad into my mouth. I guess I had to eat something if I wanted to avoid another evening like last night. The few slugs of rum I'd downed earlier was all that filled my belly. The familiar taste of something I hadn't had in years was a welcome sensation. I'd forgotten how much I loved Newfoundland food. I added a second forkful of the pinkish colored mashed potatoes.

"It was their ship. Big, but narrow. Y'know, so they could easily sneak into coves and bays that other ships couldn't. I remember your mother telling me a story about Maria. That she'd covered the stern's windows with blood, so they glowed a reddish hue at night."

Aunt Mary's words sparked an odd visual in my mind. The ship in the bottle. It was most definitely a pirate ship... and the stern's windows glowed red.

"The name came from the fact that The Cobhams never left a ship behind. After they raided one, Maria ordered to have it burned until the ashes sunk to the bottom of the ocean, with its crew aboard. Then, their black ship would disappear. Like a ghost. It went on like that for years and years until, one day, they really did disappear. For good. They dropped off the face of history. No trace whatsoever."

The old red chest called to me from across the room, like a heartbeat in my ears. The scattered mystery of it was beginning to piece together in my mind and I started to wonder if I even wanted to bring it back to Alberta with me. I looked down at the jacket I still wore. Maria's jacket, obviously, and my skin crawled. I stood and grabbed my plate, looking to Mary.

"I think I'm going to get some sleep. I'm still not feeling a hundred percent," I lied.

Mary looked surprised. "Oh? Did you need anything from the house? Pepto? Advil? I can run over and grab whatever you need."

"I think I just need more sleep, is all," I replied, hoping she'd catch the hint. I wanted to check out the contents of the chest again, by myself. "Thanks for the food, it was awesome. I'll put the rest in the fridge for tomorrow."

"Oh, okay, dear," Mary stood and threw on her jacket, "I'll come by again in the morning. Maybe we can spend the day together before you head back on Sunday."

I began walking her to the door. "Sure, that sounds nice. And I can show you what gets trashed and what the museum can have. I'll give you a hint. Pretty much all of it."

After Mary gave me the look of disapproval and headed on her way, I ran back to my cursed pirate's chest. The compass, the coins, dagger... I couldn't pack them away fast enough. Finally, I slammed the lid shut and latched the keyless lock. I figured, no need to ever open it again. Nobody should touch these things, these horrific tokens from the past. But then, I noticed I still wore Maria's red jacket and the ship-in-a-bottle still sat on the dining room table.

"Shit."

I reached for the tiny ship, but the bell-shaped sleeve of my jacket knocked it and I watched, in slow motion, it seemed, as the bottle fell to the floor and smashed. In the stark silence of the empty house, the piercing sound of glass smashing sounded like a gunshot.

I bent down to pluck the few large pieces of the broken bottle as a cloud of strange chemical-like dust wafted up from the wreckage and I accidentally inhaled it. Coughing, I stood and made my way to the kitchen to dispose of the glass and fetch a broom.

When I returned, my blood turned to ice when I glanced down at the mess. The water that had spilled from the bottle was… moving. I watched, frozen, as the small amount of liquid poured across the hardwood floor as if it were alive, making its way to the patio doors.

"What the hell?"

I took a careful step to follow it when a strange, deep rumbling incumbered my ears and seemed to come from all around me, I could even feel it under my feet. The entire house shook and a quick glance at the patio doors, out toward the ocean, told me where the sound was coming from. My heart threw itself into a panic as adrenaline sparked to life in my veins.

A massive wave came rolling towards me, tearing up the landscape outside, an unstoppable force too large to even believe if I hadn't seen it with my own eyes. I was still frozen in place, entranced by the beast. A little too late, I turned to run, but I felt the wave smash through the glass doors behind me, relentless as it quickly filled the house and sucked me into a watery abyss.

CHAPTER FIVE

My head spun, and my body protested as I struggled to open my eyes. The slight rolling motion in which I moved made my stomach queasy against the hard object that drove into it. The skin on my face felt hot, burning in the warm sun above me.

My eyes finally peeled all the way open to discover that my arms were wrapped around a strange wooden object—my pirate's chest—and it was the only thing keeping me afloat. As I glanced around, it was evident that the small tsunami had swept me out to the middle of the ocean and I bobbed there, alone, with no visible sign of land to be found.

The weight of Maria's soaked jacket threatened to pull me under, but I had to keep it on if I wanted to avoid burning in the hot afternoon sun. Out here, on the water, the sun's heat always intensified, giving you two things to worry about; the UV rays and the reflection off of the water. I had no choice but to hang on and hope someone would be out this far today and spot me.

It felt like hours had crawled by as I floated along, not knowing whether I was drifting closer or further from the prospect of land, when I suddenly heard the splash of something moving next to me. I managed to pry one of my sunburned lids open to spot a small boat, a rowboat, with two bodies making its way toward me. My eyeballs burned with tears of joy mixed with the dried ocean salt around them, but I didn't care. Someone was coming to save me.

But my joy was doused when I heard them speak.

"Is that she?" one of the men asked.

"I'll be damned. It sure looks like the wench," the other replied. Their boat came broadside of me then, and an arm reached down to pluck me from the water, nearly yanking my shoulder out of the socket. They threw me to the bottom of the small boat like a disregarded fish. "The captain will surely want to gut this one himself."

"Think he will?"

"Oh, you knows he will. I wonder where she's been all these years?"

They spoke strangely. A heavy Newfoundland accent was definitely there, but one of the men had a strong mix of Scottish. They sounded rough, and I didn't like what they were proposing their captain would do to me. Surely, they weren't serious? The strength to move or speak evaded me.

The Scottish one reached down and pawed at my wet, matted hair to reveal my sunburned face. "Gus, look at this! This ain't she."

"Well, I'll be. The girl sure looks like her, though. Could be her sister."

"Now, ye knows as well as I do, Maria Cobham ain't got no sister. And if she did, she'd surely have murdered the likes of her."

The mention of Maria lit up my senses. Who were these men? And why did they speak of my three-hundred-year-old ancestor as if they knew her? I also didn't like the idea that I resembled the sadistic woman. The very thought made me want to spew the saltwater from my stomach. A moan escaped my dried lips and I caught the faint image of a sword, some old leather boots, and dirty fabric as I rolled over, my brain threatening to pass out. I was clearly dehydrated and hallucinating.

"Grab the trunk," the one named Gus ordered. "Maybe there's something good in it."

The other man chuckled; a raspy smoker's sort of laugh. "I allow a fine lass such as she will be enough to please the captain, don't ye think?"

"Just grab the damned trunk, Finn."

***

My consciousness swam to the surface in short bursts as my body was pulled from one location to another. I remembered being in the rowboat with the men named Finn and Gus. But exhaustion ruled my body and only allowed me to recall brief images; being hoisted from the small boat, the strange and grimy wooden surface beneath my feet as they dragged my lifeless figure across it, and then the impact of my body slamming into an old barrel when the two men tossed me inside some sort of dank cell. The last sound to grace my ears was the loud metal clank of the cell door closing and latching.

I awoke sometime later, how much time, I had no earthly idea. The constant pounding in my head was unlike anything I'd ever experienced. No hangover or migraine could even compare to the deep throbbing I felt, like a massive heart beat inside it. Then, for a moment, I'd thought I had wet myself but soon realized that the floor of my dingy cell was covered in stale, murky water.

"What the Hell?" I cursed and sprang to my feet, not able to fully stand in the short cage.

The disgusting liquid moved in under the gated door. Through the metal bars, I could see out to the location where I was being held, but I couldn't bring myself to believe my eyes. Barrels stacked haphazardly along the walls, sacks of things throw against them, piles of thick rope coils, and wooden crates moaning as they swayed with the movement of the very floor beneath me.

I was on a ship.

I approached the bars and peered out, trying to find someone, anyone, to help me.

"Hello?" I yelled, my throat so dry, it hurt to speak. "C-can anyone hear me?"

"No one on The Devil's Heart can help you, dearie," an old man spoke.

He seemed to have come out of nowhere, with his giant mop, making his way across the wooden floor of the ship. He swished it back and forth but all it did was push the dirty water around. The man grabbed a rusty milk pail and dumped its contents onto the floor; more disgusting water and began to arbitrarily plop the mop around in it.

"What's the Devil's Heart? Where am I? Who are these men?" I pleaded. My cell seemed to be on a slant because all the water eventually ran toward me and pooled beneath my feet. I noted the absence of shoes as my socks and pants soaked it up. I hopped up on a crate and leaned against the metal bars in a crouch. "Who do I speak to about this? You can't just throw people you rescue in a cell. I'm not a criminal. You don't even know me!"

"Rescue?" the man chortled. "Oh, dearie, you were not rescued. You're lucky to even be alive. If it were the captain who'd found ya out on the water, wearing that jacket and havin' that hair."

"Why? Because I look like Maria Cobham?" I shouted.

The old man dropped his mop and came to the bars. "Shhh, you're alive now, don't ruin it for yourself by sayin' that name around here."

Up close, I could see the hard shape he was in, the dim candlelight highlighting his features. Dry, wrinkled skin, dirty and gnarled fingernails, missing teeth. The ones that remained were yellowed and the gaps filled with plaque. He wore strange garments, too. Soiled and worn, but I could easily see the old-fashioned cotton trousers and what was once a white men's blouse underneath a long apron. It was like I'd woken up in the past.

Where the Hell was I?

"Alfred!" bellowed a familiar voice. The old man's eyes lit with panic. "'Tis nearly noon and I dinnae smell food bein' made. Why aren't ye in the kitchen?" The Scottish man who'd scooped me out of the sea, Finn, came stomping over to Alfred's side.

"Aye, Sir," Alfred replied. "I was just getting to it. I had to finish up the deck. Swabbed it clean, I did."

Finn glanced down at the murky water that skimmed the surface of the floor. "Ye did a fine job," he said with all seriousness. "But the boys is hungry. And the captain will be sniffin' around soon. So, get to it."

Alfred nodded and scurried away, leaving his mop and bucket behind. Finn then approached the bars of my cell, his grin showing off teeth that were only slightly better than Alfred's. He'd actually be somewhat handsome if he'd cleaned himself up a bit. Greasy red curls hung down from a black bandana and pooled around his shoulders. Green eyes sparkled as they stared at me, and his face, under the dirty smudges and wiry red beard, had a cherub-like appearance.

"What are ye doin' talkin' to our cook?" he asked me.

"I-I was just trying to get some help. I don't understand why I've been locked up. I've done nothing wrong."

"Aye," he said with a nod and rocked back on the heels of big, brown leather boots, "But yer surely in cahoots with Maria. Look at ye."

I glanced down at the red coat I wore. "What does a jacket have to do with anything? I found this. It doesn't even belong to me."

He unsheathed a large dagger from his side and pointed at me. "So, ye stole it, then? Yer a dirty thief?"

My eyes widened in panic. I needed these unstable people to believe I was a good person.

"No, no, I swear. I found the chest, and the jacket was inside. I put it on and was swept out to sea. That's when you found me. I promise. I'm just—" I paused to think, amusing my delusions, "I'm merely a baker's daughter. I honestly only found the old chest and the things inside it. I'm just lost and would only like to be escorted back home, please."

"Well, that's a very convincin' story, lass," Finn replied. "But it's nae up to me what happens to ye."

"Well, who do I speak to, then?"

He chuckled. "That would be the captain."

"Okay, well, bring me to your captain."

"Nay," he said. "It dinnae work like that. The captain will decide when he wishes to speak with ye, if he even does at all. Ye may find yourself at the bottom of a watery grave before the day is out, lass." Finn turned on his heel then and began walking away.

I yanked on the metal bars. "What? Why? I've done nothing!"

"We shall see 'bout that!" he yelled over his shoulder before climbing up the short ladder to the deck above.

I retreated into my cell as far as I could, in search of a glimmer of safety. Where could I possibly be? Who were these men and why did they seem so... out of place? Why did they lock me up instead of getting some help? I crouched down in a dark, musty corner and felt something dig into my thigh. I reached inside my jean's pocket and pulled out the snow globe key chain. I could use the key as a weapon, I thought, as memories of the one self-defense class I'd taken came to mind.

I opened my jacket to put the key somewhere I could reach it better and realized I'd slipped Henry's journal inside it before all of this happened. The paper had been soaked by the ocean's water, but the inked script barely bled. So, I handled each page with gentle care, stealing glances out through the bars of my cage to make sure I was alone, and searched for the next entry, to find out what became of young Henry.

August 14th, 1698

I have come to accept my fate aboard The Burning Ghost. Maria will never let me go. I had intended for my last entry to be just that, my last. That night, I had snuck out of Maria's bed once again, the evidence of our disgusting affair still fresh on my body. I planned to stand on the bowsprit and take my own life, so my body could fall to the sea below. Where I belonged.

But, alas, one of the ship hands found me and brought me to her. To say she was angry would be an understatement. My skin still breaks open from wounds she inflicted that bloody evening. Her husband Eric still stands by, idly, without care, or notice.

But her reign of terror over my mind and body did not end there. No, Maria has moved on to other forms of torture. Since that dreadful night, she has been determined to bring me together with the devil. She calls him Devil Eyes and insists I embrace him.

I tried, I truly did, to keep a hold on my humanity. To not forget who I am... or was. But Devil Eyes is a pirate whose evil seeps into your soul. I can feel him in my veins, swaying my mind and influencing my choices. She forces me to spend far too much time with him.

Now, Maria has taken it upon herself to bring me along on longer, more brutal, raids. Devil Eyes has forced me to take seven lives and each one chip away at my soul. Soon there shall be nothing left, an empty shell for Maria and Devil Eyes to play with. A puppet.

Last night, we boarded a small vessel. It appeared to be a cargo ship transporting rice from the South. Maria had tied the crew up in gunny sacks and lined them on deck. I often watched her as she tossed men overboard, listened to them scream for their lives as they plummeted to a slow watery death. Sometimes she would use them as target practice, she's not the best shot, from what I can tell.

But last night, Devil Eyes and Maria forced me to do it. To decide if they were to be tossed overboard, alive, or if they were to be shot first. The shrivel of my past self-wanted them to have a quick death, no suffering. But she did not like that. She wanted me to suffer more than them. So, she made me do it. Maria put the pistol in my hand and Devil Eyes pointed it for me. I knew I was a good shot, my father saw to that. I cried as my finger pulled the trigger and a lead ball smacked one of the gunny sacks. A little cry rang out as the person inside squirmed and then, finally, stopped. As the bag toppled over, I realized it was not tied shut and the small, lifeless body of a child poked its head out.

That was the final straw for me. I cannot go on living like this if you call it living at all. So, this, I swear, is my last entry as Henry William White. Tonight, I will let Devil Eyed Barrett take my life and set me free from this Hell. He owes me as much.

I closed the journal and just let the tears roll down my face. Poor Henry. He was just a child. Maria Cobham, my own flesh and blood... I found it hard to believe that such evil flowed through my veins. And at that moment, I hated myself. Even though it wasn't me, and it happened hundreds of years ago, I had no right to be there on this Earth. Henry did, though. It wasn't fair that he had to die, that the Devil Eyed Barrett pirate could just take his life and Maria's legacy got to live on even to today. In me.

I rested my head against the side of the cell and closed my eyes, dreaming of what Henry may have been like. He seemed to be noble, honest and loved his family dearly. Perhaps, if we had lived in the same time, we could have been friends. We'd play down by the water and he'd take me on his tiny boat to catch squid and bathe in the sun as we held hands. I wondered what he may have looked like and pictured a post-pubescent boy with golden hair, a sweet smile. Maybe some dimples. I tried to hold on to the thought, to honor his memory, as I quietly cried myself to sleep.

***

The sun set three times before I saw any hope of getting out of the cell. Night after night, day after day, I laid there on the crate that was barely large enough to hold my body in a fetal position, watching the sunlight fade to darkness and the slight twinkle of stars poking in through the narrow opening where the ladder was positioned. I mostly laid there, listening to the sound of waves swooshing below. When the inevitable time came for me to use the bathroom, I yelled for someone to help me as I banged the buckles on my jacket against the metal bars of the cage. Finally, my other rescuer appeared, the shorter one with the dark hair and scowling face. Gus.

"What the Christ is all the racket?"

I backed up and stood tall. "I need to pee."

"And what, exactly, do you want me to do about that?"

I narrowed my gaze. "Bring me to a bathroom? Unless you want me to urinate all over the floor?"

The man rolled his eyes and turned to leave. I wanted to protest, to yell after him, but before I could he returned with a wooden pail. "Step back," he barked and fetched some keys from his belt. I watched as he unlocked the cell and tossed the bucket at me. "There you go. Now shut your gob." The door slammed shut and he locked it once more before stomping off.

I glanced down at the bucket in my hands and I would have vomited if I'd had anything worth coming up. The wooden pail had clearly been used as a toilet before, and often, without proper cleaning. I tossed it to the side, refusing to touch it. I put it off as long as I could, held it in, but I finally broke and squat over it one night when the coast was clear.

Thankfully, each morning, the cook would come and give me a dirty metal tray with some stale bread and something that resembled broth. I begged him for answers, to help me, but he ignored my pleas and went on his way. On the fourth morning, though, he finally spoke.

"They're coming for you today," he whispered through the bars as he handed me my tray, casting shady glances over his shoulder.

"What does that mean? Are they going to kill me?"

"I don't know," he replied. "I overheard some of the men speaking with the captain when I brought him breakfast. They were deciding what to do with you, and the captain ordered to have you tied up and brought to his quarters."

My heart squeezed with panic and my stomach rolled. Why did I have to be tied up? It wasn't like I could run anywhere. We were on a God damn ship. Unless...

"W-who is your captain? What is... what would you think he'd do to a woman who was tied up?"

The chef's faced drooped and I could see he felt bad for me, he knew my concerns. "They call him Devil Eyed Barrett, one of the most ruthless men on the sea."

That wretched anvil dropped in my stomach at the sound of his captain's name. The same name I had found in Henry's three-hundred-year-old journal. How could that be possible? Was I really in the past? Could that ship-in-a-bottle have been, I shuddered at the idea of admitting it to myself, *enchanted*?

"I've never known him to harm a woman, but I've heard of the vile things he's done before I was brought aboard." He stopped to heave a sigh and move in closer. "I say this with sincerity. If you do not give him what he seeks, then you best pray for a quick death."

"Alfred," I whispered, "Can you tell me what year it is?"

He appeared confused but gave a slight shrug. "Of course, miss. The year be 1707. August month."

The impossibility of my situation sank in and my mind threatened to check-out. I'd somehow transported myself back in time, just nine years after Henry was captured by Maria and Devil Eyed Barrett. And now... now I was aboard Devil Eyes' ship. I reached through the bars and wrapped my hand around his thin wrist.

"Please, I beg of you. Let me out. Point me to a boat and you'll never hear from me again."

The sound of heavy footsteps approached.

"I must go," he said and fled away to the shadows of the ship.

Finn and Gus came toward me then. When comparing the two shipmen, Finn's red hair and tall, broad figure towered over Gus who was shorter, stumpy, with a mess of brown curls that matched the scraggly beard that hung from his face. Both the men had sheathed swords that swung from their hips and Gus held a bundle of rope in one hand, no doubt meant for me.

"G'marnin', wench," Finn greeted humorously as he slipped a key in the large metal lock of my cell. He heaved on the door and it swung open with a screechy creek. "'Tis time for ye to meet the captain."

I backed away, retreating further into my cell. "Why do I need to be tied up?"

The two men exchanged a cheeky grin and Gus replied, "Oh, for our protection, of course."

"And my name isn't *wench*," I spat, "It's Dianna."

They threw themselves into a fit of laughter.

"Ooo! I'm sorry, m'lady," Finn mocked and then took a little bow. "Shall I prepare some tea and have a dress fluffed and ready for ye, as well?"

Gus grabbed my arms and brought them together behind my back. "Your name means nothing here on The Devil's Heart. And a woman on the sea is a bad omen. The sooner we get rid of ya, the sooner we can get back on course."

He tied my wrists together and the rope burned my skin as he yanked it tight. Then the two men removed me from my cell, led me toward Devil Eyed Barrett, and possibly to my death.

If I were lucky.

CHAPTER SIX

I got a taste of what their ship really looked like as Gus and Finn hoisted me up the ladder and dragged me across it. It seemed as though my cell had been located on the deck near the center, surrounded by piles of rope and stacks of crate and barrels. When I glanced back, I realized my cell wasn't even a cell meant to contain prisoners. It was a place to hold goods because three ship hands immediately began tossing the gear and items back inside it.

But there was a message in their actions. They had no intentions of putting me back in there. I truly was going to die at the hands of ruthless pirates. A cold sweat broke out all over my body and pooled in unsightly places. Days of being in the cell had taken a toll, my hair and skin smelled as bad as it looked. Not that any of it mattered.

We stopped in front of the large door of the ship's stern, wooden and hand-carved with intricate details of vines and strange symbols. If any movie or TV show taught me anything, this is where the captain's quarters usually were. Finn banged on the door and waited. My heart thumped hard against the inside of my chest and then squeezed tight when a voice bellowed from the other side, telling us to enter.

Gus opened the door and Finn grabbed the knot that held my hands together, pushing me inside. The space was surprisingly large and far too tidy for a pirate. A massive desk with wooden claw feet anchored the room, its surface covered in scrolls, maps, and strange metals objects.

A bed could be seen off to the right and nestled in a nook, red velvet curtains hung down and were pinned off to the side. Book filled shelves towered above our heads, almost as tall as the large stern windows that lined the back of the room. My eyes then landed on a figure standing in the sunlight streaming in, facing the sea. Captain Devil Eyed Barrett, in the flesh.

"Captain," Finn addressed, "We brought her, as requested."

The figure, still with his back to us, replied, "Very well. Leave us." The deep, raspy sound of his voice raised every hair on my body. They'd brought me to the devil's den.

The two men turned to leave but I panicked. "Please!" I cried, "Don't leave me here. You can't do this! I don't deserve to die!"

They exchanged a glance and then burst into a fit of laughter before leaving me, closing the door behind them. I stood there, staring at the door, frozen stiff, my body refusing to do anything. My back was to the room and I could hear Devil Eyes' clunky boots walking toward me. Try as I might, my lungs wouldn't inflate enough to take a deep breath and my chest moved with short, tiny breaths. A hand touched my ratty hair and gently pulled some of it back before running fingers down the sleeve of my jacket.

"Are you scared?" he asked with the smallest hint of a British accent.

Of course I was scared, and I was betting he knew it. But now was the time to establish where I stood.

"No," I answered, my chin held high. "Should I be?"

The captain let out a hoarse, guttural laugh and I nearly jumped out of my skin. The sound of his footsteps retreating gave me the courage to turn around and I found him leaning over his desk.

He was tall, much taller than Finn, even. An all-black leather ensemble dressed him from head to toe, the only contrast was his long, white-blonde hair that tied back at the nape of his neck, under the captain's hat. Finally, he revealed his face as he peered up at me from the desk, and I understood why he was named Devil Eyes. His gaze pierced through me like two black holes, threatening to suck me into oblivion.

"That depends," he replied.

"On?"

I watched as the captain picked up a metal device, no doubt used for reading maps, examined it between his fingers and then pointed it at me. "What you did with the bottle."

Crap. "I-I don't know what you mean."

He tossed the item back down on his desk and glared at me. "You're lying. Strike one." He then unsheathed a dagger from his side and examined the tip. "Where is the ship in the bottle?"

That's really what he wanted? Out of everything in that chest, he wanted the darn trinket? "I don't–I can't tell you. I don't have it."

He circled the desk and sauntered toward me, the dagger swinging between his fingers. "What would you say if I told you your life depended on it?"

I narrowed my eyes at him while my hands strained to wiggled free of the rope ties. "You'd seriously kill someone over a stupid toy?"

He closed the distance between us, leaving nothing more than breathing room, and held the dagger's tip to my throat. Those black eyes just inches from my face. "I assure you, it is far more than a mere toy."

I swallowed hard; the simple movement caused my skin to brush against the sharp tip of his blade. The pungent smell of tobacco and wine assaulted my nose. "Well, perhaps if you untied me, we could sit like civilized adults and discuss it. I can't think straight when I'm bound and threatened at knifepoint."

Devil Eyes let the blade slide down my throat, scraping the skin as it did. He never took his eyes off mine and I could see then that they weren't truly black. They were just such a dark brown that, with the pupils, appeared to be big and black. He leaned in even closer and reached around me, his face nearly touching mine, and my heart beat wildly for fear of my life.

But I was surprised when the captain grabbed my wrists and spun me around. The sound of his dagger slicing through the ropes and the relief of my hands being freed was refreshing and I turned to face him again, rubbing my wrists to help the circulation come back.

The captain began walking over to a small table with two chairs that sat under the stern's window. "Come," he ordered, and I scrambled over, "Sit down, then. And you can tell me all about where you hid The Burning Ghost."

Wasn't that Maria's ship? I tried to swallow again, but I was just way too dehydrated.

"Here," he added with a heavy eye roll and scooped up a metal pitcher.

Devil Eyes poured me a glass of what looked like red wine and I sat down across from him to drink it. I was right, it was wine, and it burned my salt dried throat. But I didn't care. It was wet.

"The Burning Ghost?" I repeated, eyeing at the tray of fresh bread and dates over the rim of my cup.

He sighed impatiently and pushed the tray toward me. "Yes, the ship."

I shoved two dates in my mouth and lobbed off a chunk of bread. It actually wasn't that fresh, but it was heavenly compared to the cardboard they'd been feeding me the past three days.

Between chewing, I replied, "Why would someone want to make a model of such a horrible boat?"

My question caused a surprise on his face that caught me off-guard.

"You think it a horrid vessel?"

I shrugged. "Well, yeah. I mean, Maria was a monster, wasn't she?" His lack of response gave me the opportunity to keep going. I had to gain his trust somehow if I wanted to stay alive. "Unless you're still working with her? Then I would understand if I've offended you with that comment."

His eyes widened in horror. "How do you—"

"Listen," I cut to the chase, "I don't know what you think of me, but I bet it isn't good. What, with me showing up wearing this jacket, her chest clutched in my arms. But I promise you, it's all a coincidence. I only found it, I swear. I put the jacket on, I looked at the stuff inside. I never meant to break the bottle, but I did, so—"

He shot up from his chair as if I'd electrocuted him or something. "What did you say?"

"That it's a coincidence—"

He grabbed his dagger again and spiked it into the table just inches from my hand. "No, about the damn bottle," he demanded, furious.

"I-I broke it," I told him. "I'm sorry! If it was of any value I'll... pay you back?"

He removed his hat and tossed it on the desk, then began pacing nervously. "You stupid *woman*!" he yelled at me. "How could you be so careless? You've no idea what you have done!"

"I'm sorry, it was an accident," I pleaded, "how was I supposed to know it belonged to someone?"

The captain stopped and looked at me, a realization falling over his vulnerable expression. "Yes, you're correct, you had no idea. Nobody knows..." he spoke, seemingly to himself and stared off into the distance.

I don't know why I felt sorry for this man, this person who was just as much a monster as Maria, according to Henry's journal. But I did. He looked absolutely distraught over the breaking of the bottle. Maybe it was a memento from his days with Maria? Maybe she gave it to him as a gift or he was supposed to keep it safe or something? I wondered then if they'd been romantically involved. Obviously, Eric never cared what she did.

"I'm really sorry for breaking your ship in a bottle," I approached him slowly, "will you... will there be repercussions for it? Will you get in trouble or something?"

Devil Eyed Barrett turned to me, his eyes glossed over. "Oh, my dear, we're all in a world of trouble if you truly broke that bottle."

I shook my head in confusion. All this over a dumb trinket? "But why? What's going to happen?"

He laughed, the kind that crazy people let out when they can't think of any other way to react. "The Burning Ghost was trapped in that bottle, with Eric and Maria aboard it. By breaking it, you've set them free to wreak havoc on the world once again."

Now it was my turn to laugh. "You can't be serious," I replied, "Why would you think that?"

Captain Barrett downed an entire glass of wine, then grabbed the rope that had tied my hands and came toward me with a fierceness in his soulless eyes. "Because I put them there."

CHAPTER SEVEN

It seemed like hours had crept by since the captain bound my wrists and tethered me to his desk. The damn thing weighed as much as an elephant. I had tired myself out within the first ten minutes, trying to pull free. So, now, I just laid there, half on the floor, half against the desk for that was all the slack the ropes allowed.

I could hear lots of yelling from outside, people bustling by and things being moved about. The ship even turned around, from what I could tell, and we now sailed off in some other direction. I tried to wrap my head around what the captain told me. That The Burning Ghost, the *real* ship, had been trapped in that bottle. It seemed like a grim fairy tale. But, then again, how could I explain the wave that crashed through my house and brought me here? It was all tied together by some sort of old magic I'd never understand. I still wasn't sure if I even believed it.

The door burst open and people came pouring inside. The captain, Finn, and Gus crowded around the desk above my head. They completely ignored the fact that I was even there, tied up and on the floor like a dog. They didn't even respond as I squealed when one of their heavy leather boots caught the ends of my hair and pinned my head down further. I listened to them fussing with the papers and maps I saw earlier.

"Where would they go?" Finn asked.

"I'm not certain," the captain replied. "They could be anywhere on the West Coast."

"Well, where were you when you put them in the bottle?" Gus chimed in.

More ruffling of paper. "Here. The Burning Ghost was anchored at Sandy Point in this flat bay area. Martha and I approached from the base of the isthmus and she performed the spell. I suspect it would be safe to assume that's where the bottle would release them."

"Aye," Finn said, "So, we stay on this new course, head back up to the West Coast and kill the buggers."

"But how do we find out exactly where they are?" Gus asked and then moaned. "We still have that delivery to make, too. Probably best to do it along the way. If they've been free since her arrival, then they've a good head start on us."

The three of them glanced down at me, fury in their eyes. I could feel their hate and disgust for me filling the air around us. I single handily brought back a monster. I set the evil beast free. They were definitely going to kill me. But then... did it even matter? I realized, if they were on a course to find and kill the Cobhams, then I would cease to exist at the very moment their swords drew.

I glanced up from my spot at their feet and locked eyes with the captain as he answered them. "Easy. We follow the trail of blood and ash."

***

I remained bound and tied to the captain's desk, only now I was alone. The sun had set, and darkness filled the room, just a gleam of moonlight highlighted the surface of the objects in the space. I cried, quietly, and grieved for my family. Not just my mom, but my entire lineage back to the Cobhams. By breaking that bottle, I accidentally changed the course of history.

Mind you, it wasn't an important history in terms of the world, but it was important to me. When the crew of The Devil's Heart find and kill Maria, they'll be wiping out half of my family's entire existence, myself included. I wondered if I would fade away like in the movies when something happens to alter time, or would my body actually die here in the past. Either way, I remained, so the new past had yet to catch up with my future. That is to say... if time was even linear.

Once again, the door flung open and heavy footsteps barrelled toward me. Finn then bent down next to where I sat, and he grinned through the gruff red beard. "I reckon yer hands are damn near dead by now."

"Does it matter?" I replied. "You guys are going to kill me, anyway."

The Scotsman sighed. "If we wished ye dead, we'dve fed ye to the sirens long ago."

I gave him a hopeless smile. "No, you don't get it."

"Aye," he replied and began releasing me from my ties. "Probably not. But I dinnae care. I'm here to bring ye to a bunk."

I stood when he did, rubbing my poor wrists once again, the skin chaffed and bleeding. "A bunk? You mean, to sleep? I don't have to be tied up anymore?"

"Well, we'll keep an eye on ye, but there not be many places ye can flee to," he kidded. "May as well put ye to work."

"Work?" I asked, afraid of what that would entail, me being the only female on a ship of burly pirates.

"What skills do ye have?"

"Uh, I can cook," I told him, hoping it would be of use. "I was a very good chef back—" I stopped myself from saying the future, "back where I lived."

"We have a cook," Finn told me, "Alfred. He ain't very good, but he keeps us fed. I dinnae see the captain letting ye replace him. Alfred isn't exactly a skilled sailor."

We were on deck then and Finn led me across the surface. I glanced up at the masts above us, they were like giant tree trunks with massive white sails pulled taut as the wind pushed us toward our destination. I counted four deckhands; one in the crow's nest high above, and three tending to the many ropes and levers down here on deck.

They eyed me with such hatred. One of them even spit at my feet as I walked past. I was the wench that brought evil down upon the world again. The reason they had to change course. They said something about going back up to the West Coast, which told me they must have been heading South. Maybe somewhere warm. Or perhaps they were on a hunt for treasure. Whatever the case, I ruined it and they despised me for it.

We descended a small ladder to the deck below where a dozen wooden tables filled most of the space; six on each side that were built-in and fastened to the ship. A buffet-style counter sat at the front where I also spotted a wood stove, washbasins, and various barrels that no doubt contained their food. This was the cafeteria, or whatever the pirate word was for it. Mess deck?

Finn looked at me. "This is where we eat. I'll bring ye back up in the marnin' for some grub." He grabbed my arm. "Come on, then. This way."

We descended another ladder to the next lower deck, this one clearly reserved for sleeping. The space was lined with hammocks and dirty sacks of clothes were thrown about. Some of the crew members were sleeping so I remained quiet. The stench of sweat and other nasty things was almost unbearable. My stomach heaved, and my eyes watered as the odor filled my nostrils.

Finn just laughed. "Aye, it's not the prettiest of places to rest ye head, but I reckon it be better than hogtied at a desk."

"I beg to differ," I whispered.

He perked an eyebrow at my forwardness and I regretted the insult. "Well, perhaps cleaning the lower deck shall be ye first job." He stomped over toward an empty hammock, larger and wider than the rest. "This is where ye shall be tonight. Be grateful for it. I could have slung ye in with Maurice."

My eyes followed where he pointed and saw an unsightly old man who seemed to be the human form of the disgusting space and he grinned at me. Not a friendly grin, either. No, he eyed me with a hunger I hoped I'd never have to satisfy and I made a mental note to stay away from Maurice.

"Are you just going to leave me down here with..." I swallowed hard and glanced around at all the pirates I had yet to come to know. Not that I really knew Finn, but I had a sense of trust in him. However slight that may be.

He chuckled quietly. "Nay, I'll be restin' me head right next to ye. This be my hammock." He hopped in and slipped his boots off the side. "Ye best not snore, neither."

I nervously wrapped my jacket tightly across my torso and slowly eased my body into Finn's hammock where I slid right up against him. He was warm, and my spine immediately thanked me for the relief. The nights spent curled up on a crate and the hours tied up on the floor left me aching. But, tired as I was, I couldn't bring myself to close my eyes next to this strange man whose body mushed against mine.

I felt him shift and froze as I felt his lips come close to my ear. "Ye dinnae have to worry, lass," he whispered carefully. "As beautiful as ye may be, I dinnae fancy the curvy body of a woman."

I turned my head, so my eyes could meet his and found him grinning like a child who'd just told me the location of their secret hideout. "You mean—"

The coarse skin of his palm covered my mouth. "Don't mistaken me friendliness for compassion. Ye tell anyone what I just said, and I'll gut ye myself."

I didn't reply as he shifted his body again, so we were pretty much spooning. "Now, g'night, wench."

***

I woke the next morning, disoriented, but well-rested. At some point during the night, Finn had wrapped his giant limbs around my body and held me close like a teddy bear. My bladder sprang to life and immediately protested, but I couldn't move a muscle. The burly Scot had me trapped.

I wriggled and tried to wake him. "Finn. Finn, you're crushing my body."

He moaned, and I felt his body tense as he stretched. "Aye, sorry. Ye was having nightmares and I couldn't sleep next to ye flailin' about like that."

"I was?"

"I reckon," he replied as he rubbed his face and yawned. "Moanin' and cryin'. Ye just about flipped us over, too."

"Crap, sorry," I told him. My bladder squeezed again. "Um, I have to, uh—"

"Take a piss?"

I cringed. "Yes, is there a restroom aboard?"

"What the Christ is a restroom?" he asked, pronouncing the words as if they were foreign. Which, when I thought about it, probably were to him.

"Like, a place to, y'know?"

"Aye, a place to take a shyte and piss." He rolled off his side of the hammock and straightened himself out. "Come with me, lass."

I copied the way he got out of the tipsy bed and followed him over to the corner of the lower deck area. A torn and soiled curtain hung from the ceiling and created a half-circle around a sketchy looking bucket.

"Here ye go," he said and motioned to the bucket. The smell wafted up to my face and I knew then where the majority of the room's stench came from.

I looked to Finn, eyes wide in fear. "You can't be serious?"

"As serious as a blade in the back, lass." He turned and faced away from the make-shift restroom. "I'll stand guard while ye do yer business."

Sitting on that bucket was the last thing I wanted to do but I had to pee. What else would they offer if I refused? Hang me over the side of the ship? I mustered up the courage and hover-squat over the bucket. "Could you at least sing or something, so we don't have to listen to me pee?"

He laughed but, thankfully, began to hum a Gaelic tune. After I was done, Finn led me to the ladder and up out of the lower deck. The change in the atmosphere, cleaner and thinner, was glorious after a night spent down there. I sucked in as big a breath as I could manage, letting the fresh air fill my lungs and noted the heavy scent of food.

The mess deck was alive with the breakfast crew and they all stopped to stare at me. Suddenly, I was extremely aware of how I looked; frazzled, dirty, and totally out of place on a ship full of men. I remembered something that Gus had said before. Women were a bad omen on the sea. I made a note, then, to watch my back. My life could end in a split second if left alone with a superstitious sailor.

"Aye, what are ye all gawkin' at?" Finn growled. "Ye all never seen a woman before, or what?" He put a hand on my back and pushed me toward a table near the front where Gus waited, his food not touched.

"About time you both got up. The day's half gone," Gus said by way of greeting.

"G'marnin' to ye, too," Finn replied and then looked to me. "Sit. I'll grab ye some grub."

I slid my butt onto the wooden bench seat, across from Gus, and nervously fiddled with my hands under the table. "Good morning."

He scowled. "We shall see."

I didn't know what his problem was. He despised me from the moment they plucked me from the sea. But the tiny Englishman didn't scare me.

"What's your deal?" I asked him. He looked confused and I remembered that I had to stop using modern lingo. "Why do you hate me? I've done nothing to you. I'm a good person, I swear."

"I don't much care what you are," he replied. "But you make the captain uneasy. I've never seen him fuss about the way he has since you were brought aboard. As Quarter Master, it is my duty to worry for him. If he doesn't like you, then neither do I." He then opened his jacket to reveal a pistol and dagger, letting me know not to do anything stupid. I just nodded.

So, Gus was the ship's Quarter Master. I knew that was, like, assistant manager, or something. I wondered what Finn's job was. They were always together with the captain, so it was of some sort of importance. If I were to survive and try to fix the mistake I created, then I had to win over these two men. Finn was easy, and I knew his secret. However, Gus was a mystery.

Finn came back with two bowls of a pale, lumpy slop and two lobs of stale bread.

"Eat," he ordered and slid one serving in front of me.

I glanced down into the bowl and stirred the questionable substance with the silver spoon.

"What is this?"

"What's the matter?" Finn blurted out between chews. "Ye ain't never seen porridge where ye come from?"

My eyes widened in surprise. "Oh, no, I've seen porridge. I make a delicious one, actually, with brown sugar and raisins and a sprinkle of chopped walnuts." I licked my lips and then glanced down. "But this is not porridge. This is… watery goo. I can't believe you eat this."

The two men exchanged curious glances.

"Where did you say you were from, again?" asked Gus.

Startled, I fought to find words. "The mainland?"

"Where on the mainland?" Finn added.

Just then, the cook came over to our table and laid a tray down next to us. "Good morning."

My handlers smiled and tipped their heads. I copied them.

"I trust you slept well, miss?"

"Yes, thank you," I replied and cast a sideways look to Finn who was grinning behind his chunk of bread.

"What's our course?" Alfred asked the two pirates.

"The captain thinks we may find the Cobhams by week's end, if they be where he thinks," Finn told him. "Then I reckon blood will be shed."

Alfred looked distraught, but I saw how he quickly hid his expression, masking it with a fake smile. "Would you gentlemen be so kind as to bring the captain his breakfast? He refuses to leave his quarters again today."

Now I was the curious one. "Why won't he leave? Is he okay?"

Finn opened his mouth to speak but Gus cut him off. "Now, that be none of yer business, wench."

"Look, my name is not wench. It's Dianna," I yelled at the pirate. He looked taken aback at my sudden forwardness. But I'd had enough. Seriously. These were all rough and tough pirates, they were being ridiculous. "I know about *good* porridge," I risked a quick sideways glance at Alfred, "because I am an exceptional cook. And yes, I am a woman. On your ship. But that doesn't mean I'm bad luck. Get over yourselves, you're supposed to be a bunch of men. Not a bunch of sissies." I stood to leave and swiped my stale bun. Better to have something in my stomach, and there was no way I'd even try that slop.

But Finn grabbed my arm. "Not so fast, lassie." He stood to meet me and scooped up the tray of food that Alfred brought over. "The captain awaits."

"No need, Finn," a deep, raspy voice spoke from behind us.

I cranked my neck to find Captain Devil Eyed Barrett standing at the base of the ladder, all decked out in his black leather, and he started toward us. Now that my brain had a chance to settle and process my new reality, I could look at him with a clearer view. The dark, terrifying eyes, the intimidating outfit, and the way he carried himself... he was everything I dreamed a ruthless pirate would be.

But he was also unbelievably handsome. My eyes scanned the jagged line of his jaw and admired the beastly broadness of his shoulders. Devil Eyes was the epitome of a Harlequin Romance novel hero. Only... he was no hero. He was a monster. The very monster who'd killed sweet Henry.

Everyone stood in respect as their captain made his way over to our table. "Sit," he ordered, and they obeyed. He stopped next to Finn and looked down at the food tray he held, a look of pure disappointment clear across his face. He hated the slop just as much as I did.

"Captain," Alfred hastily butt in and grabbed the tray from Finn, "Let me warm this up for you."

Devil Eyes forced a smile and a curt nod. "Yes, that would be wonderful, thank you."

As Alfred scuttled off back behind his counter, the captain took a seat next to Gus, refusing to even throw a glance my way. Was I that terrifying? What threat could a single woman possibly pose on a ship? I played along like a child, not looking at him, either.

Instead, I cast my eyes over to Alfred who appeared to be acting strangely. Only a few men remained down on the mess deck, the rest were up top and tending to their duties, so no one really paid attention to the strange cook and he didn't notice me as I watched him fiddle with the captain's food; scooping the porridge back into a warm pot, his eyes flitting around the room nervously.

Then, to my surprise, I saw him pull a small vial from his apron pocket. The manner in which he handled it, with care and secrecy, told me it was something bad. Alfred grabbed the steaming pot and dumped the slop back into the bowl, then quickly poured the contents of the vial in with it. I realized, then, what he was doing.

He was poisoning the captain.

Panic filled my veins and threw my heart into overdrive. I had two options in front of me. Sit back and say nothing, allowing this man to commit murder in front of my eyes. It would save the Cobhams and, by extension, save my entire lineage.

Or I could stop him.

I argued with myself as Alfred carefully carried the tray back over to our table. He set it down in front of Devil Eyes and slowly backed away, an evil grin smeared across his face. I couldn't believe what I was witnessing. But the good person inside me took over my body and I threw myself across the table, knocking the tray and the spoon full of slop right out of the captain's hands.

Within seconds, the pirates in the room had me surrounded and Gus grabbed a hold of my arms, securing them tightly behind my back. Devil Eyes stood and came toward me, his massive stature towering over my mundane frame, anger alight in his black eyes.

"How dare you!" he bellowed.

"How dare I?" I choked out. "I just saved your life. Alfred was trying to poison you!"

The group of pirates appeared confused but turned to their trusted cook for answers.

"The woman is clearly deranged, captain," he told them. "Why would I do such a thing?"

"It's true! I watched him pour a small vial of something into your porridge."

Alfred narrowed his beady eyes at me. "She's lying, captain."

Devil Eyes drew his sword and held the tip to my neck. "Prove it."

"Prove it? How am I supposed to do that?"

Just then, two rats came scuttling out from underneath the tables. I watched as they sniffed around the spilled slop and one of them began to eat it.

"Ha! There!" I blurted out like a crazy person. But the pointy tip of the sword pressed harder against my skin, so I told myself to calm down. "The rats.

They're eating it. Just wait. If they die, then you'll know."

The men looked down at the rodents feasting on the poisoned food, unaware that the cook began to back away toward the ladder. Where did he think he could run? Within a few seconds, the one that took the first nibble began acting strange, a coughing sound erupting from its belly. It keeled over, its death quick and swift, and a resounding gasp made its way around the room. Captain Barrett looked to Alfred.

"Alfred," he said, sadness in his eyes. "Why?" The cook said nothing in reply and turned to scamper up the ladder. "Seize him!"

Finn leaped across the room like a redheaded giant and grabbed a hold of the man, yanking him down from the ladder and pinning him to the floor. "What do we do with him, captain?"

Devil Eyes looked to me, a strange mix of emotions shimmered across his face. Regret. Anger. Something else. "Death is the only answer for this treason. Tie him up and bring him on deck."

Everything happened so fast, I'd barely had a chance to process my thoughts. I saved a man's life, but I damned another one to death and still didn't save myself. The crew of The Devil's Heart was still on course to find the Cobhams and kill them, inadvertently ending my entire lineage and sentencing me to a death I had no idea how to imagine.

I hung my head low while the men led me up on deck and stood around as Alfred, bound and tied, was made to stand near the side of the ship. Devil Eyes pulled a clunky pistol from the opposite side his sword hung from and pointed it at the former cook. Everyone stared at Alfred, but I looked at the expression of the captain's face. He appeared tormented. Like it pained him to have to take this man's life, even though the man tried to kill him.

"Alfred Cummings," Captain Barrett spoke loudly, "For your treason against your captain, you are sentenced to death. Do you have any final words?"

Could no one else see the hesitation in their captain's actions? I stood and saw a man who clearly didn't want to take a life, the internal battle plain across his face. But, one quick glance around at the crew, hungry for blood to be spilled, told me all I needed to know. They wanted justice, and Devil Eyes had to provide it. No matter the cost.

The man held his head high and grinned evilly. "May you all be met with the flame of The Burning Ghost." Everyone gasped at the mention of the cursed ship. "And never—"

A loud explosion pierced the air and rang in my ears. I let out a scream as I watched Alfred's body go rigid, stumble back, and then fall to the ocean below. The crew, oblivious to their captain, erupted with a loud cheer and danced about, but my eyes were fixated on the man who appeared as frozen as I was. His glossed eyes met mine and, for a brief moment in time, I felt his pain. It shot through me like a blunt sword and filled my body. How could this man be the monster depicted in Henry's journal?

He turned away from the crew and walked toward his quarters, stopping at my side first. He said nothing, but his furious eyes locked onto mine and held a warning within them. He left me there, adrenaline and fear coursing through my body as I listened to his footsteps nearing his door. I was beginning to think I had Captain Devil Eyed Barrett all wrong. And now I wanted nothing more to figure out what was right.

CHAPTER EIGHT

I wandered the ship for a while, waiting for the captain and his two right hands to discuss some things. It wasn't a huge vessel, but a decent enough size for the dozen or so crew members. Everything was dank and musty, which was to be expected on a ship, I guess. A salty film had crusted over the surface of certain areas, and each deck harbored a dreadful stench, getting more concentrated the deeper I went. I finally decided that the top deck was where I liked it best, open and breezy. I stood at the side near the bow and gazed down at the hypnotizing water below.

How did this happen? How did my mother come to own enchanted things and never know? She would have loved this, minus the life-threatening situation. Just then, one of the crew members found me and approached slowly. A young man with a sweet face.

"You're not thinkin' about jumping, are you?" he asked me jokingly.

"Oh, God no," I replied. "I can't imagine how cold that water is."

We both laughed awkwardly, and he sidled up next me, leaning his forearms on the ledge. "Are you really who they say you are?"

"I don't know," I answered, confused. "Who do they say I am?"

"Part of *her* crew."

"You mean Maria?"

His eyes bulged, and he glanced around. "Jesus, watch what you say."

"Is she really that terrifying?" I asked. "And, to answer your question, no. I'm not with her, from her crew, or associated with her in any way." I swallowed hard as I realized that was a lie. We shared the same blood, after all.

"Some say she was a plague sent down to Earth to torture the men of the sea. Others say she was an abomination, something… not human. When she disappeared, there was a strange calmness that cast over the sea."

I nodded, my gut toiling. "And now I've let her loose again."

The boy frowned. "Yes, you've got a target on your back. I'd lie low if I were you."

I thanked him, and he ran off across the ship.

A while later, I had taken the young man's advice and found a spot to lie low. I sat in Finn's hammock, the lower deck empty of crew members. I pulled Henry's journal from my inside pocket, curious to know more about the Captain Devil Eyed Barrett. But I worried that there would be no more entries, no more evidence of Henry's life. He was so set on ending it and so certain Devil Eyes would be the one to do it. But, if the captain had a difficult time shooting a man who tried to kill him, how could he possibly kill an innocent boy?

I fingered through the pages, gently peeling them from each other, but I found nothing but empty whiteness. I followed through to the very last page, hanging on to any shred of hope that Henry lived. But, as I turned the last blank piece of the journal, my eyes filled with tears. That was it. He was gone, and I'd never really know what became of him.

I wrapped the book with its twine and stuffed it back in my inside pocket where I would protect it until I could one day put poor Henry to rest. Maybe I could find a nice open meadow and bury it. It was the least I could do for the young man who captured my heart in a few simple pages. His pain was almost tangible. I curled up and attempted to fall asleep but a loud thump on the deck floor alerted me to someone's presence. I cranked my head in the direction of the ladder and found Finn coming toward me.

"I'm here to fetch ye," he told me.

"And bring me where, exactly?"

"The captain," he replied. "To determine what to do with ye."

I flipped out of the hammock and stood in place. "They won't kill me, will they?" I pleaded. "I saved your captain's life."

"Aye, but ye cost us our cook."

My eyes widened. "Are you seriously that ignorant? If I didn't do what I did, you'd all be without a captain and, who knows, maybe he would have killed the rest of you."

"Aye."

"Aye?" I squawked. "All you can say is *aye*? Finn, please, surely, you're smarter than that. I *know* you know I'm a good person. I mean no harm."

He rolled his eyes and grabbed me by the arm. "Just come with me, will ye?"

I followed him to the captain's chambers where we were met with Devil Eyes and Gus. These two really seemed to be the only ones the captain surrounded himself with and I was glad for the glimmer of friendship Finn has shown me. Maybe it would play in my favor.

Finn closed the door behind us and the captain stared at me. Gus stood off in a corner, arms crossed like a contrary child who didn't get his way, refusing to even glance in our direction.

"Dianna," the captain spoke, the sound of my name felt strange on his tongue. "Please, sit." I did as told and took a chair across from him at his desk. "You've left us in quite a predicament, with no one to feed us. What are we going to do about that?"

"Look, I saved your life. If you can't be grateful for that, then just kill me now," I cut straight to the chase. "I'm dead anyway," I added under my breath.

But he seemed to catch it, a look of surprise smeared across his face and he leaned back in his chair. Silence filled the room as the captain and I engaged in a stare down. His black eyes bore holes into my head as he seemed to be trying to read my mind or something. I just refused to be the first to look away, but it gave me a better opportunity to admire his devilish good looks. I'd like to think that his terrifying presence made him repulsive, but it only added to the allure of him. Devil Eyes was like a dark enigma, a black hole that threatened to hypnotize me and draw me into his secret.

Finally, he broke the silence. "Finn tells me you're a cook."

"Captain—" Gus spoke up, but Devil Eyes threw up a hand to stop him. Gus retreated to his corner in a huff.

"Well, are you?" he asked again.

I looked to Finn, standing just a few feet to my left, and he urged me with his eyes to say yes. I realized then, he must have vouched for me. While they left me down in Finn's bunk, they must have been here, arguing about what to do with me. Obviously, Gus wanted me gone but, thankfully,

Finn had a soft spot and the captain had half a brain.

"Yes," I croaked out, "I am a very good cook, in fact."

"Excellent," the captain clapped his hands together, "It is settled, then. You shall take Alfred's place as the ship's cook as well as tend to the swab duties with one of the deckhands." Gus was stewing, pacing behind the captain over near the stern's large window. "Do you accept?"

"Henry!" Gus finally broke, but the name he used knocked the breath out of me.

The captain stood from his chair and turned to his quartermaster. "How dare you use that name," he spoke with a stern warning, "I understand your concerns and have taken them into consideration. But, I am your captain, Augustus. Know your place."

The Englishman sighed and nodded, then bowed his head in shame.

Devil Eyes came, sat back down, and began speaking to me but his words deflected from my ears. My mind was traveling down a muted tunnel and all I could do was stare at the pirate across from me with a mix of both awe and sadness. But also with a new pair of eyes. It was like a layer of him had peeled away and I could envision the sweet little boy who loved his parents. The young man who'd been captured by pirates and sentenced to a life of terror and abuse. Henry truly did give his life to Devil Eyed Barrett.

He became him.

"Dianna!" he said, his voice raised and impatient.

I snapped out of my trance. "Sorry, I... what?"

"Do you accept the role of our ship's cook?"

Just moments before, I would have struggled with an answer. But now I wanted nothing more than time to talk to the captain. To get to know the man of the boy I read about. I had so many questions. "Yes," I answered, finally, "yes, of course I'll cook for you."

I heard Finn let out a heavy breath and he stepped closer to me. "Aye, lass. Ye had me guts in a tizzy for a second there."

"What? Why?" I asked him.

"I put me neck out for ye," he explained. "Gus wanted to toss ye overboard. But I thought it a waste. Ye said ye could cook. I like to eat. I thought it was a good enough reason."

I smiled at my new friend, the big and burly Scotsman. He was a hard man to dislike. Despite his massive size, Finn had a soft warmness about him. Perhaps it had something to do with his sexuality. Who knows? I was just thankful for the turn of events. If I had Finn's favor, and now the knowledge of the captain's true identity, perhaps I could earn their trust and convince them not to kill the Cobhams. Maybe there was a chance I could save my lineage.

"Thank you, gentlemen," Devil Eyes said. "You can leave us now."

"Aye, captain," Finn nodded and motioned for Gus to follow him. After they left, I remained in my seat across from Devil Eyes, unsure of what to do or say. Or what to expect. It seemed he felt the same as we entered a strange, drawn-out staring contest.

"I assume you have questions," he finally spoke.

I chortled. "You have no idea."

"As do I." He stood and made his way over to the table under the window and scooped up a tray. "For starters, how did you know I spent time aboard The Burning Ghost?" He came back to me and laid down the tray that held a silver teapot and two cups. I watched as he filled them with tea and stirred in the sugar cubes.

"What do you mean?" I answered and accepted the warm cup when he passed it to me.

"When we first spoke, you asked if I were offended by your comment about the vessel because of my connection to it."

I backtracked everything in my mind and replayed the events of the last few days with a fresh perspective. He said he was the one who'd trapped the Cobhams in that bottle. Which means... Henry trapped them. Henry never died, he'd found a way to live with the man Maria forced him to become, and he found a way to defeat them. But to answer the captain's question would mean trying to explain time travel, to which I had no proof.

Unless...

I carefully opened my jacket and reached in to pull out the journal. Henry's journal. I placed it on the desk in front of me and the captain's eyes widened in horror. Then, slowly, his face softened with acceptance.

"I wondered where it went," he said quietly. "You had the jacket, and found the bottle, obviously." He then turned his gaze and I followed it to the chest that floated me back in time. It sat on his bed, open.

"How did you get it open?" I asked him. "I locked it. And there's no key."

He grinned and picked up a large brass key from the desk. "Simple. The chest, it belongs to me." He stood from his chair and walked over to the small trunk. "I don't know why I held on to the key. After I escaped The Burning Ghost, this chest held all that I owned in the world. But also held everything that reminded me of *her,* because she'd given most of it to me."

I swallowed hard. "Of Maria?"

Devil Eyes shot me an angry look, as if the very sound of her name pained him. "Yes, Maria. I had no idea evil could manifest in a human form as it had within her. She was a monster. Heartless. I convinced myself that if I'd cut her, if I could make her bleed, nothing but blackness would seep from the wound. Like a disease."

"So, why didn't you kill her?" I asked. "Why trap her and Eric in a bottle?" I couldn't believe the words that came out of my mouth, that I was amusing the idea of that sort of magic existing.

"I wanted to, I truly did. It's all I think about. Even now, to this day." He sighed and came over to me, stopping at my side to pick up his journal. "But she didn't deserve such a swift ending. She needed to suffer for eternity."

I saw my chance. "So, why kill her now? Why not put her and Eric back in the bottle?" I looked up at the man that Henry had become and admired his strength. But I wondered why he remained a ruthless pirate. Why continue a life of piracy after you've defeated your enemy?

Unless he was too far gone.

"It was only by chance that I found the witch who performed the spell years ago," he told me. "There's no guarantee I'd ever find her again. She remains hidden. Protected."

"But why not try?"

"You simply cannot understand my reasoning. I cannot exist in a world where she roams free."

I glanced down at his trembling hand and he quickly slipped it behind his back.

"I think I understand a little. I mean, I read the journal."

Stone cold silence hung between us, clinging to the walls and shrouding us in an awkward bubble and I wondered if he would kill me for what I knew.

"You think me a weak man?" he asked after a while. In that moment, the pirate I'd feared the last few days was gone and all that remained was little Henry, scared and alone.

I had no idea what compelled me to do so, but I reached across the table and softly, carefully, placed my hand over his. "No, I don't think you are or were a weak man," I told him with certainty. "The complete opposite, in fact. To live through what you did... to still be half a human being, functioning—"

"Nobody knows," he said, blurting it out as if the weight of the secret had been killing him.

"You mean, nobody knows who you are?"

"They've no idea of my time on The Burning Ghost," he replied and finally met my gaze.

"Seriously?" I whispered. "But, I don't get it. What do they think is your reason for wanting her dead?"

Henry grinned, but it didn't meet the sadness in his eyes. "My dear, Dianna, every pirate on the sailing seas wishes to end the Cobham's reign of terror. They hunt every ship within reach. But they have a thirst for pirates."

I nodded in understanding. "So, your crew thinks you're just doing your duty as a pirate, what any of you would."

"Yes, all except Gus," Henry added. "He knows very little, but more than the rest." He paused, and his expression changed to worry and a hint of anger, his eyes narrowing. "But not more than you."

I swallowed hard as a cold sweat broke out under my arms, my heart straining from the stress of the constant bursts of fear. Fear for my life. The boy I read about in that journal was long gone, and I had no idea of Devil Eyes' mental stability. He could kill me in a second. Especially now that he was aware I knew his deepest, darkest secret.

"Henry, I swear, I will nev–" Before I could finish, he grabbed me by the arm and forced me to my feet, then led me to the door. I tried to pull free, but he kept a firm hold, rough and painful with no regard for my body. "Henry, please! What are you doing?"

A forceful yank on my arm brought me close to his chest so our faces met, and the warmth of his breath splashed across my face. "Do not *ever* call me that aboard this vessel." His eyes were wild with anger and desperation.

I continued to be dragged across the ship's deck and over toward the edge where Alfred fell to his death just hours earlier. Suddenly, I realized what was happening and a fight-or-flight response set in. I struggled against Henry's hold, but he was like a freaking bear.

"Please! No!"

It was no use. The crew came toward us, circling in and getting ready to watch the next show. Henry grabbed me by the waist, his two massive hands like a vice, and hoisted me up on the railing.

"You know too much, Dianna," he said low enough for only me to hear. "We need to do something about that."

My voice evaded me, so I pleaded with my eyes, to tell him that the secret was safe with me. I'd never tell a soul. I would cook their food and keep my head down. But all I received in return was a devilish grin as he leaned into my face.

"If you're going to stay aboard my ship, then you need a bath," he whispered in my ear, his breath tickling my skin. With arms wrapped around me, I thought, for a moment, that he was hugging me, but soon realized that Henry had tied a rope around my waist.

My eyes widened with a new fear, no longer for my life. But before I could form a response, Henry gave me a shove and I fell to the ocean below. Even though it was the middle of summer, the deep-sea water was still freezing cold and the chill hit my body like an electric shock. I clawed my way to the surface and gasped desperately for air. The force of the waves swooshed my body around as the ship dragged me along. With the breath still knocked from my lungs, I felt a hefty tug at my waist as they finally began to hoist me back up to the ship.

My stomach threatened to heave the very little it contained as the thick rope dug into me. Every tug acted like a weird Heimlich Maneuver, the last couple of yanks rubbing a little too hard against my bottom ribs. Captain Barrett pulled my body over the side and let me fall to the floor like a large fish and I coughed up the saltwater I'd sucked in through my nose and mouth.

I peered up at the men who stood around me, laughing at my expense, but I stopped at the captain and narrowed my eyes. He wanted to scare me and it worked.

"You could have given me some warning, you know."

He let out a gusty laugh. "Now, where would be the fun in that?" He strolled over to me and bent down, scooping me up like a drenched ragdoll and putting me on my feet. "Come, I'll get you some dry clothes." We both headed toward his quarters as he yelled to the crew, "Get back to work. We should meet landfall in three days time."

Once inside, he closed and locked the door behind us. I couldn't stop the shivering that took over my body and the saltwater still burned the cavities of my nose and throat.

"I'm sorry for that," he told me. "But the men needed something entertaining after this morning's events." I watched as he rummaged through a large chest next to his bed. He pulled out a white blouse and a pair of black trousers, then turned to me and grinned. "And you did require a bath."

"I thought you were going to kill me," I replied and accepted the dry clothes from him. I tried to shrug out of Maria's jacket, but it was soaked and heavy, and I was too cold.

"May I?" he asked. I hesitated, but then nodded, and he proceeded to peel the drenched coat from my body and then hung it on the back of a chair to dry. "And I wouldn't kill someone without a damn good reason."

"I just thought... because I know your secret."

Our bodies were so close, and I was extremely aware of the cool air and the absence of a bra under my soaking wet tank top. Henry's eyes averted to my chest, taking note of the view. I self-consciously covered my breasts with my free arm and took a step back.

"Just to be clear. I'm to provide meals for the crew. *Nothing* more." Henry didn't reply, only kept his hard gaze on my shivering body, then slowly moved his stare up to meet my eyes. "A-are we clear?"

Finally, he nodded. "Yes, of course."

When he turned away, I quickly changed out of my wet clothing and slipped on the dry ones. They were far too big, but I didn't care. They were warm and dry. I grabbed the key chain from my jacket and the belt from my jeans, tightening it around the trousers, then tied the bottom of the blouse together in a knot at my waist.

"You can turn around now."

"Very good." He straightened his jacket and adjusted his black leather hat. "I have some things to tend to, but you're more than welcome to stay here while you finish drying and warm up. There's fresh wine and bread on the table. But don't take too long, the men need feeding and dinner soon approaches. You must pull your weight around here." Before he reached for the door, his hand came up to my face and held my chin a little too tightly. "And I'm well aware that you know my secret, Dianna. Do not mistake my hospitality for mercy. If you breathe a word—"

I shook my head. "No, I won't, I swear."

His grip on my jaw tightened with aggression and he leaned in close, our noses touching. "Good. Because, if you do, there won't be a rope tied around your waist next time."

CHAPTER NINE

After Henry's warning, I desperately wanted to gain his trust. I had a sliver of it, but I wanted more. I needed it, especially if I were to convince him not to kill The Cobhams. I quickly adjusted to my new role aboard The Devil's Heart and found comfort in duties.

I cooked and cleaned while constantly on the lookout for Henry, hoping to catch glimpses of him but he very rarely left his quarters. I daydreamed about what he must have been like in those early days after he'd finally escaped The Burning Ghost. Days went by in a blur and I was grateful we had planned to meet landfall soon because the meager food supply I started out with grew smaller by the day.

I found all the tools required to cook, but as far as food went... a bag of flour, a tub of butter, half a sack of stale oats, a few satchels of what I assumed were baking powder or something, a crate of old potatoes and carrots mixed together, and some dried fish was all I found. Most of that was gone in the first two days and I had a crew of a dozen men to feed.

On day three, I wracked my brain to think of something for lunch and found a near-empty jar of molasses at the bottom of a crate. Then it dawned on me. The perfect idea. And easy, too. I began to sift together the basic ingredients for an old bread recipe my mom taught me. One that didn't need yeast.

I fired up the stove and placed a massive cast iron pan on top to heat up. It wasn't long before I had a massive basket full of freshly made fried bread, an age-old Newfoundland favorite. Henry's favorite, from what his journal told me.

There wasn't enough molasses for everyone to share, but I doubted the crew would have anything to say about it. Before lunchtime rolled around, a few whose names I'd yet to learn came sniffing around and took their seats in anticipation. When the mess deck was full, I laid out a stack of plates on my counter next to the basket of toutans.

"Dig in, boys," I said loudly.

They raced to the front, pushing one another out of the way, and grabbed handfuls of the dense pancakes. I felt a slight sense of pride that I managed to please a large group of men with such skimpy ingredients.

"These smell good enough to eat," Finn told me with a wink. He had three in his hand and then stuffed one in his mouth. "Ye keep cookin' like this and the crew will love ye in no time."

"Thanks, Finn," I replied and stuffed one for myself in the front pocket of my apron. Then I grabbed the tray meant for Henry and made my way up the ladder. I knocked on his door but didn't get a reply. Thinking he was maybe asleep, I snuck in to place the tray on his desk.

"What are you doing?" a voice bellowed from a far corner.

I let out a shriek and nearly dropped the tray. "Jesus! Don't do tha–" But words escaped me when I realized he was getting dressed. He'd managed to shove on his trousers, but his torso remained shirtless as he stood and stared at me.

Henry's angry eyes fell to the tray I held and his face softened. "Is that..."

"Toutans," I replied, holding the tray out toward him. He walked over and stopped right next to me. His half-naked body made my pulse do crazy things and I forced my brain to formulate words. "Your favorite?"

Henry examined my face with strange scrutiny and then smiled, the first one I'd seen reach his eyes. "The journal."

"Yeah, sorry," I told him. "I didn't tell anyone down below if that's what you're worried about. I just did my job, cooked the food, and left them to help themselves." I laid the tray down on his desk. "And I'll leave you now, too."

"Wait," Henry spoke. I turned back around. "Would you… eat with me?"

My brows raised in surprise. "Seriously?"

"Yes, please. I often eat alone. It would be nice to have some company for a change."

I peered down at my dirty apron and slightly less dirty appearance.

"I don't–" My breath caught while Henry reached around my shoulders.

My body froze as his fingers brushed the skin of my neck, moving my hair out of the way. I should have backed away, I should have told him to keep his bloody pirate hands to himself. But I couldn't bring myself to say it, to say anything. He terrified me. But, the big, burly, chiseled pirate before me… I didn't know that I would have argued if he took me in his arms and demanded my body. And I was sorely disappointed when I realized that he was just removing my apron as he untied the knot at the back and tossed it aside.

"You look perfectly fine to join me for a meal, Dianna," his raspy voice caressed my ears and I felt my nipples harden.

What was wrong with me? I caught him quickly glance down at my chest, where my body deceived me, and I hastily crossed my arms. Henry just grinned and walked over toward his small dining table, grabbing a white blouse from the back of his desk chair as he did.

The two of us sat across from one another in silence as Henry divided up the stack of toutans I'd brought. My stomach was in knots. I didn't like the feeling that he was attracted to me, that he could take me if it pleased him to do so because he was used to just taking what he wanted. Being a pirate, and all.

But another part of me twisted in a knot at the realization that... I wanted him to. He was mysterious and dangerous, with a dark and tortured past that only I knew about. It made me feel special but also fear for my life. Sure, he showed an interest now, but he could turn on me in a second if he felt that his secret was going to be exposed.

I watched as Henry drizzled the molasses over our plates and my mouth watered. "Eat," he ordered.

I waited, to see his expression when that first bite met his tongue. I fished for those slight moments, the ones when he'd drop the rough and tough pirate façade and let his expression soften.

"My dear, Dianna," he spoke through chewing, "these are to die for."

"Thank you, I'm glad you like them." I relaxed and then tore off a piece with my fork and shoved it in my mouth. I let out a slight moan. "God, I forgot how good these were."

"I as well," he replied. "Such a simple dish but so satisfying."

I nodded and continued to pile it in my mouth. I had been starving, with nothing more than a few bites of bread and watery broth over the last few days. "That reminds me," I spoke up, "Did I hear we're going to meet landfall today?"

"Yes," he answered hesitantly, "Why do you ask?"

"Well, if I'm going to keep cooking for you guys, I'm definitely going to need more to work with. I mean, as awesome as these are, I doubt the crew will survive off fried bread for long. I need quality ingredients."

I was surprised to find that Henry appeared... relieved. Did he think I was going to run away when we met land? Now was my time to establish some more trust. "You can send one of the men with me if you want. To... keep an eye on me?"

He seemed to mull it over, examining my face for any sign of deceit.

"I won't know where to go, anyway. Probably best if I don't get lost," I added and gave him a wink. He brightened, and it aroused an odd sense of joy in my gut.

"Yes, probably best not to get lost," he agreed, "we cannot afford to lose two cooks in one week."

We continued to eat, letting a comforting silence hang between us. Occasionally, I caught him staring at me, but his eyes would flit away. When I'd finally felt full, I laid my fork down and blew out a deep breath.

"So, do you know where to find them?" I asked.

"Who?" Henry replied, setting his fork down and wiping his face with a napkin.

"The Cobhams. We're reaching land today, is it because you know where to find them?"

"No."

Good. That meant I still had time. And, according to every science fiction movie I'd seen, the fact that I still remained meant that the actions of the past had yet to catch up with my future.

"We are stopping for supplies, a good night's rest, and to suss out the word on land."

"The word on land?"

"Yes, if The Cobhams have been mucking about, there's bound to be whispers on land. We may get a sense of where they are."

I nodded in understanding. Then something else he said came to mind. "So, we're staying on land overnight? Like, in a real bed?"

The thought made me weak in the knees. I was beginning to despise hammocks. Especially ones I had to share with a giant Scotsman.

Henry chuckled. "Yes, we'll take rest in a nearby tavern for a night or two."

I stood and began clearing the plates, stacking them back on the tray to bring back to the kitchen.

"I'm sorry about the accommodations aboard the ship. But there are no extra hammocks. Finn suggested you bunk with him for... obvious reasons."

I stopped and rested a hand on my hip. I had worried a little for my safety as a woman aboard a ship full of men but never knew for sure if it should be a real concern. "You mean to protect me from getting raped? Is that seriously something I have to worry about?"

The captain stood, his massive stature towering over me, and I tipped my head to meet his gaze. "Not if I can help it," he answered. "I've told the men to keep their hands off you."

I chortled. "Wow, I can't believe this." But I had to remember the era I was stuck in. "And how well do they listen to you?"

His black eyes narrowed. "They *will* listen." But there was a hint of uncertainty in his voice.

"Great," I spat, and scooped up the tray, "I guess I'll just go back to work and try not to get raped."

Henry's massive hand grabbed me by the waist and swung me back toward him. The nearness of the man made my head spin with conflicting thoughts of danger and desire. "If anyone is to touch you in a manner you deem unfit, then they shall be met with my blade and a watery grave. Do I make myself clear?"

A shaky nod was all I could manage. My eyes were locked on his mouth as he spoke the words. I had to pry my mind away from wanting to close the short distance between us and touch my lips to his.

When my eyes averted upwards, I found a similar yearning mirrored in his expression.

I pulled away from him. "Yes, thank you."

I secured my shaky grip around the tray's handle and grabbed my apron before leaving. I couldn't get away quick enough but the further I got the more I could think straight. *Get it together, Dianna. You're not here to get involved with a damn pirate. Gain his trust and save your family. Then find a way to get home.*

But the tightness in my chest and the fluttering of my heart never ceased as thoughts of Henry refused to leave my mind. I was in a whole new world of trouble.

CHAPTER TEN

We made landfall later that evening, shortly after suppertime. I didn't bother to cook as the crew had been boasting about the feast they would indulge in once we got to the tavern. I was thankful because it took me the rest of the day just to clean up the kitchen and wash their dishes. They were like a bunch of slobbery children. But I didn't mind. It gave me something to do. A purpose.

Captain Barrett had assigned Finn to watch over me during our time on land, and he would be the one to escort me around to get all the ingredients on my list. The captain refused to even look at me, even when he handed Finn a small satchel of coins for me to use, he spoke through him, not directly to me.

I made no secret of my distaste for the way women were treated in this era. My constant eye-rolling and frustrated sighs never seemed to register with them, for which, I was somewhat grateful for. But this time... I'd offended Henry somehow, or made him feel uncomfortable. Or perhaps he was ashamed of the attraction he felt for me. I did, after all, look like Maria. Either way, it bothered me.

The thirteen of us filed into The Thirsty Trout, a local tavern in the small coastal community we docked at. The ceilings were low and the floors waved with the uneven foundation. Some walls were built of stones, some of logs, and a large staircase led to the rooms above the eating area down below. The place was near empty aside from the innkeeper. The captain walked up to the front desk as the rest of us hung back and waited.

"My good man," Henry greeted, as he sauntered up to the front desk, his long, black leather jacket swaying behind him. "My crew and I wish to rest our heads here for two nights if you have the accommodations."

The innkeeper lit with joy at the sudden burst of business. I was betting sailors and travelers kept most taverns such as this afloat. "Yes, of course," he happily replied and bent to fetch the keys from behind the desk. "I have eight rooms free, so you'll have to bunk up with each other."

Henry nodded. "Of course." He scooped up the keys and turned to the men. And me. "Pair up, some of you have to share." He handed Finn and Gus their own keys. Then Henry looked to me, and I thought he might ask if I would share his room but Finn, thankfully, cut in.

"Aye, Lassie," he nudged my arm, "yer bunkin' with me, right?"

I smiled and nodded awkwardly, but I caught the look on Henry's face before he turned back to the innkeeper. It wasn't a happy one.

"We'll retire to our rooms and get cleaned up," he told the man. "What time shall we expect supper? Or did we miss it?"

The old man looked startled. "Oh, dear," he replied. "Please, I beg your forgiveness, Sir. But our cook is ill. We've no one to man the kitchen this evening. But he should be back in the morning, for breakfast. I'll see to it."

A mutter of curse words made its way through the crew as they dragged their feet toward the staircase. Finn peeked at me from the corner of his eye and flashed a wicked grin across his bearded face.

"Finn, no–"

"Aye, there be no missin' a meal t'night," he bellowed. "We have a fine cook right here." He grabbed me by the shoulder and crushed me tight to his side. "Dianna will be happy to man yer kitchen."

All eyes were on me and no one said a word. The innkeeper looked hesitant but clearly saw no way around the offer.

"I mean, if you'll let me," I added.

***

I stood in a decent sized kitchen with all the supplies and ingredients I needed to make a delicious meal. But it was getting late and the crew would no doubt be sniffing around soon. But what could I make in an ancient kitchen that wouldn't take forever and a day? At the restaurant back home, one of the easiest, most filling, and tastiest dishes was always pasta. My go-to. But I couldn't...

I took stock of my ingredients once more. "Flour, water, salt, eggs, tomatoes, milk..." I could make a pasta dish. They'd probably have no clue what it was, but one bite and they wouldn't care. I rolled up my fluffy sleeves and got to work. While my giant mound of homemade pasta dough sat for thirty minutes, I began preparing my sauce. Before long, I'd whipped together the biggest pot of pasta and rose sauce I'd ever made. And, no doubt, it'd be gone in the blink of an eye with the crew I had to feed.

Hopefully.

I suddenly worried that they wouldn't like it. Maybe they were used to their meat and potatoes and disgusting gruel. In the midst of my little internal breakdown, the old innkeeper entered the kitchen.

"Good Lord," he said and let out a whistle while adjusting his spectacles, "My kitchen has never held such glorious smells. What on Earth are you cooking, dearie?"

My cheeks flushed with color. "It's a little something from..." I paused thoughtfully, "Italy. Would you care to try some?" I handed him a small bowl.

I watched with anticipation as he removed his tiny glasses and examined the foreign food with curiosity, dug his fork in, then stuffed a scoop in his mouth. His head tilted back, and a delighted moan escaped his lips. "Well, this is just delightful. Where did you learn of such a creation?"

"I'm a professional cook," I told him. "Back where I came from."

His brow furrowed. "Then how in God's name did you end up on a privateer ship cooking for the likes of those boys?"

I shrugged. "It's a long story." But then I caught a particular word he said. "Wait, did you say privateer?"

The innkeeper appeared puzzled. "Yes, the ship you sailed in on. Your crew. I've had them here before. They're privateers. You don't know the men you work for?"

I tried my best to hide the surprise I felt. "Oh, yeah, of course." Then turned and busied myself with a bit of clean up. "I forgot. I'm new. Just started yesterday, really." It wasn't a bold-faced lie.

The man threw another couple of bites in his mouth before handing me his bowl. "Well, you'd better get this served, dearie. I hear them comin' down the stairs."

After he was gone, I scrambled around to gather a stack of bowls and headed out to the dining area. It was basically cafeteria-style tables, long and narrow, built of wood and positioned in two rows. The crew of The Devil's Heart all sat patiently awaiting their meal. They lit up like kids on Christmas when they saw me. My eyes searched for Captain Barrett, but he was nowhere to be found.

"Aye, lassie," Finn greeted, "What have ye got fer us? It smells like nothin' I ever smelled before."

I finished handing out the bowls and gave him a playful smile. "You'll just have to wait and see. It's a surprise, a special dish from… Europe."

I listened to their whispers of curiosity as I made my way back to the kitchen to grab the giant pot of pasta. When I returned, my heart nearly stopped when I found Henry, suddenly appearing at the table next to Finn and Gus. He managed a quick look but averted his eyes to the bowl in front of him. I started with their table, I wasn't sure, but I assumed the higher ranks should eat first.

Surprisingly, Gus was the first to comment. He peered into his bowl and then looked up at me, begrudgingly. "What the Christ is this?"

With an exaggerated eye roll, I replied, "Just eat it. You can thank me afterward."

The men erupted with a loud roar of laughter and it was all I could do to hide the grin as I continued to serve them. When the last bowl was filled, I headed back toward the kitchen, still more than enough pasta left for seconds, even thirds, when Henry grabbed my arm.

"Fix yourself a bowl and come sit with us, won't you?"

My pulse quickened. "Uh, sure," I replied.

Our eyes met, his obsidian gaze locking on mine and, for just a second, I was frozen. When he released my arm, my body thawed, and I scampered off to the kitchen. After I caught my breath again, I searched around for a mirror. Settling on the underside of a silver serving tray, I attempted to make myself more presentable. I untied my hair and let the mess of black curls fall around my shoulders. Then, with a quick splash of water on my face, I toweled off and headed back out with my bowl of pasta in hand.

It gave me an unexpected sense of pride when I found the crew filling their faces, hardly allowing a breath between bites. When I came into the room, a few of them stopped long enough to look up and give me an approving grin. They let out a resounding "aye!" and I felt my cheeks fill with color. Finn was right, I could win them over with food.

I took my seat next to my friend, across from Gus and the captain. "Do you guys like it?"

Finn stopped shoveling the pasta in his mouth and threw his arm over my shoulders, embracing me in another rough squeeze. His big red beard held remnants of sauce as he spoke. "It may look like a pile of guts, but 'tis the best damn thing I ever tasted."

Just then, the innkeeper came out with a rolling cart full of handled mugs and two large pitchers. "You boys must be thirsty," he said loudly, and the crew erupted in yet another resounding "aye!"

As the old man began pouring the mugs and handing them around, I realized the drink was ale, and the crew were downing it like water. Soon, they began to sing a tune I had never heard before, but the melody seemed familiar. Like most old Newfoundland songs. The innkeeper pulled out a fiddle from thin air and joined in on the fun. I just sat quietly and ate my spaghetti, very aware of Henry's eyes on me.

I wanted him to trust me. I wanted us to be able to speak freely. But there seemed to be this strange hostility between us. Perhaps it stemmed from the unexpected attraction I knew we felt for one another. I couldn't imagine the torment he must feel, admitting his attraction to a woman who resembles a monster from his past. And me... well, I didn't want to give in to my body's urges, I couldn't possibly get involved with a three-hundred-year-old pirate when my mission was to eventually go back home.

No need to complicate my situation even more.

But I was weak. And my newly-found knowledge that The Devil's Heart wasn't a ruthless pirate ship, but a privateer vessel, put Henry and the crew in a whole new light for me. I didn't know a ton about it, but I did know that privateers were secretly hired by government and military or something, to carry out acts of warfare. They weren't out there to raid the seas, they were meant to help lay the law and keep the peace. If it were true, then Henry and his crew were not bad people after all. I stole a quick glance up from my food toward Captain Barrett and the second our eyes met, his flitted away.

"So, Dianna," Gus spoke, and the three of us perked our heads up. "Where is it you said you came from?"

"The mainland," I told him for the second time.

"Whereabouts, exactly?" he continued to press.

"Here and there." I put some food in my mouth in an attempt to stifle the conversation.

"And what were you doing here in Newfoundland, then?" he added curiously. "On Crown land."

I'd forgotten that Newfoundland was part of England's rule until the mid-1900s. Technically, I wasn't even in Canada at that moment. "My mother was from England, she migrated here and married my father before I was born. So, I often come back to visit family." That's about as vague as I could get.

"What did you say your maiden name was?" Gus insisted. But my stomach clenched at the question because that was one I could never reveal. See, my mother kept her name after the marriage, and I took it when I was born. My father was a Sheppard. But Mom was a Cobham… and so was I.

So, instead, I shot him a cheeky grin. "I didn't."

Finn had enough of the interrogation and slammed his hand down on the table. "That be enough glabberin' yer mouths." He downed a swig of ale, "Let us drink!"

After an hour or so, the crew had consumed more ale and pasta than I thought humanly possible. Some locals had filed in, something they probably did on a regular basis since the tavern appeared to double as the local bar, too. I sat back and sipped on a single mug of beer, my stomach happy to be full of delicious food, and I watched the crew with a newly-found affection. They were a cheerful bunch, and I never noticed how young some of them were. A couple were no more than mere boys, breaking the boundary of pubescence. I caught Finn over in a corner, his arm draped over another man's shoulders, a local man, and the two appeared to be engaged in a private conversation.

Music, laughter, and good, strong ale filled the tavern and for the first time since I'd washed up in this era, I'd felt a sliver of happiness. Then, Henry appeared at my side.

"The men are fed and happy," he pointed out and let a pause hold the space between us. I just nodded and sipped my ale as he fidgeted nervously with his hands behind his back. "Well, then. I'll be retiring to my room for the evening." Was he hinting for me to come with him? "Can I leave you here and trust you won't flee?"

My fluttering heart came to a screeching halt and I narrowed my gaze. "Really? You're worried I'm going to run away?"

He scowled. "Well, I—"

"No, *Captain*, I'll stay right here," I assured him, my words holding a double meaning. "You can be sure I won't run off in the night in a community I know nothing about, miles from home and nowhere to go. I'm not that stupid."

More scowling. "I never meant—"

I hopped down from the tabletop which I sat on, patted his shoulder, and said, "Have a good night, Captain," before heading over to the crew. I could hear his clunky boots stomping up the stairs as I sidled up next to Finn who'd broken away from his new buddy.

"I never saw the captain get in such tizzy since the likes of ye came aboard," he told me.

"Really? So, he's not always that moody?"

"Aye, he be on the quiet side, usually," I watched him slug back a nearly full mug of ale before continuing. "Broody and the like, but never so angry."

I moaned. Great, I made the mentally unstable pirate angry. My mission was going to be harder than I imagined. How could I possibly get what I wanted, to convince Henry to change his mind, without giving him what he desired? It didn't matter that, deep down, I wanted it, too. I found myself more and more attracted to Devil Eyes, and part of me wondered if I could avoid it much longer.

Just then, a slightly tipsy Gus came sauntering over toward us with a pitcher in hand. He topped up my mug and raised the pitcher in the air. "To Dianna!" he yelled, and I couldn't hide the surprise on my face if I wanted to. "For we shall never be hungry so long as we have the wench."

I opened my mouth to protest but stopped myself. It was the closest thing to kindness he'd shown me since I showed up and, even though he was drunk, I'd take it.

With my mug raised in the air, I shouted, "Here, here!"

Then men all came to a halt, an awkward hum buzzing in the air around us, but they soon broke out into a cheer and the fun resumed.

Finn tousled my hair as if I were a child. "Yer one of us now, lassie."

Just days ago, that thought would have worried me. That the crew would take me on as one of their own, with no chance of escaping. But right then, at the moment, surrounded by a bunch of merry men singing songs, a warm fire burning and endless pitchers of strong ale... I felt something I hadn't felt since I was a child.

I felt at home.

The night continued for hours. I felt dizzy from being passed around as a dance partner, song after song. My legs were like jelly and a sticky sweat stuck to my skin. I lost count of how many mugs of beer I drank, but I knew it was nowhere near that of what Finn and Gus consumed. We drank, we sang, and we danced until we could no more. Eventually, the locals went home, and members of our crew had retreated to their rooms. I climbed the large, creaky wooden staircase to the room Finn and I shared, eager to crash before I got sick. I fiddled with the old iron handle and pushed the heavy door open, but was startled to find a large, naked Scotsman passed out in our bed with his long arm cradling a local man.

Crap. Guess I wouldn't be sleeping there tonight. I gently closed the door, careful not to wake them, and snuck back downstairs. There was a nice seated bench in the bay window of the lobby, and I curled up there for the night. My head spun once I laid down but, before long, I'd passed out.

My boozy brain slept and wandered dreams of vivid colors. But it didn't take long for it to settle on a fantasy of Henry. He laid my naked body down on a sandy beach as the warm sun shined down on us. He smiled and hovered above me, his gorgeous blonde hair blowing in the ocean breeze.

I ran my hands down his broad and chiseled body, but the sensation of touch wasn't there. It was like my hand went right through him.

"Henry," I whispered through a slight moan.

"Shhh," he replied, but his mouth never moved. As if the sound was coming from somewhere else. "Dianna..."

My sluggish brain fought to find the sound. I swam to the surface of my conscience, and my eyes opened to find the dark lobby of the tavern. Two hands slid under my body and my heart sprang to life when I realized who it was.

"Henry," I breathed.

His mouth pressed to my ear and goosebumps scoured my body. "I told you not to call me that." He continued to hoist my body into his shirtless arms. "What are you doing down here? Let me bring you to your bed."

I shook my heavy head. "Can't. Finn has company."

He stopped, seemingly unsure of what to do. "Oh, very well, then."

I didn't want him to put me down, I didn't want him to go. My body took on a mind of its own and I reached up to touch his face, pulling it toward me. He hesitated, slightly, but I knew he'd give in. His mouth came within a hair of mine and hovered around the outside of it, our noses caressed, and a deep guttural growl erupted from his body. Henry's arms tightened their grip around me and he fled upstairs to his room.

It was similar to the one I meant to share with Finn; quaint, dimly lit by candlelight, and held a bed covered in patchwork quilts. The pirate set me down and turned to close the door where he remained, hesitating to turn around. I didn't want him to think about it too much, I just wanted us to give in to the attraction we felt for one another, just for one night. No one had to know, and we could forget about it in the morning when the sun came up and the veil of moonlight and strong ale lifted.

I watched as his naked back moved with deep breaths and I stepped closer, running my trembling hand over its smooth skin. My very touch made his body stiffen and he stood straight before turning to meet me. I didn't think I'd ever get used to his sheer size, almost a foot taller than my own five and a half feet, and his wide shoulders that could wrap themselves around my body and make me disappear.

Henry watched me with blazing intensity, his black eyes unblinking, as I removed my clothes and let them pool around my feet. His breathing quickened, and he grabbed my neck, bringing our faces together where our lips danced but never touched. My body shook as Henry's warm mouth trailed across my jaw and down my neck, and I thought I'd lose my damn mind if he didn't take me then and there.

I failed to stifle a moan, but my mind spun from his touch. "Henry..."

The sound of his name deepened the intensity and he grabbed my legs, fingers digging in, the pain sending shocks of pleasure through my center. The pirate lifted me up and my limbs wrapped around his waist like a snake forcing the life from its prey. His fingers twisted in my hair and then gave a little tug, so my head swung back, and our faces met.

"I told you not to speak that name, *Dianna*." There was a hint of playfulness in his words, and he spoke my name with a deep, raspy purr. "When will you listen?"

I pressed my forehead to his and grinned. "Make me, *Henry*."

The beast of a man walked over to the bed with me still wrapped around his waist and laid us down. His fingers still entwined in my black curls, he tugged on them once more and finally brought his mouth to mine in a kiss so passionate and intense it caused me pain.

He broke away for a moment, leaving me gasping for air, only to whisper in my ear, "Gladly."

CHAPTER ELEVEN

I awoke the next day, the blaring morning sun hot on my face, and the events of the night before came flooding back to me. Henry laid next to me, far away in a deep sleep. I paused for a moment to admire the softness in his dreaming face, how the wear and tear of piracy washed away and all that remained was a sweet and handsome man. I wanted to reach out and caress his jawline, to press my lips to it. But I slipped out of his bed like a ninja and gathered up my things before I snuck out the door.

In the hallway, I stopped long enough to shove on my trousers and blouse before heading over to Finn's room. I gave a quiet knock first, then heaved the door open a crack.

"Finn," I whispered.

I noted that his companion was gone so I slipped in and closed the door behind me. I tried to rouse him from his deep sleep, but nothing worked. I bet the crew would be sleeping their monster hangovers off for most of the morning, so I turned and left with a sigh. I wanted to go to town and gather my supplies but had no idea how to get there, and I also told Henry I would go with someone.

I glanced at the big clock at the foot of the stairs. It was early. I could sneak out, get my supplies, and be back before the crew was even awake. How hard could it be to find the marketplace in a small community, anyway? So, I set out and wandered.

It didn't take long to find it. The town consisted of one main road and a bunch of smaller ones that veered off it. But the main road led to the heart of the community where I found a nest of tables and tents, people bustling about, and the smell of fresh codfish. With large satchels hanging from my shoulders and a wooden crate full of smaller supplies, I'd managed to get most of the items I wanted to stock the ship's kitchen. My arms full and weighed down by it all, a kind gentleman called out to me.

"Miss," he called from his merchant tent. When he caught my gaze, he motioned me over. As I neared, I saw that he sold trinkets, unlike most of the other merchants who boasted food. "You look like you need some help."

I smiled. "Oh, thank you. But I couldn't ask you to. I'm staying at The Thirsty Trout, I wouldn't want you to leave your tent unattended for that long."

I watched curiously as he bent behind the counter and then emerged with a small wagon towing behind him. "Here, use this," he said.

"Really? Are you sure?"

The kind man nodded. "Yes, of course. Just leave it at the Trout, I'll come by later to pick it up." Not taking no for an answer, the man began grabbing my items and filling the wagon.

"Thank you so much," I told him and then spotted something in his tent.

A small jar turned on its side, a delicate ship inside. I walked closer to get a better look and saw that the ship bore a resemblance to The Devil's Heart and a grin splashed across my face. It was too perfect. I had to get it for Henry.

"How much for the ship-in-a-bottle?" I asked the merchant and fetched my satchel of coins from my pocket.

"Now, put your money away," he told me and scooped the bottle from his table. "I prefer to trade."

"Oh, I don't really have anything of value," I replied. "Are you sure you won't take coins?" I saw him eye my wrist where a small silver chain hung. It was a birthday gift from John and I hadn't even realized I still wore it. What better way to get rid of it? I unclasped the bracelet and held it up for the merchant. "But I do have this. It's real silver."

The man's eyes widened. "Real silver?" he confirmed and shook his head. "It's far too valuable. The ship is not worth it, dear."

"Please, I insist," I urged him, "It was a gift from a man who betrayed me. Its value means nothing to me. I'd much rather have that ship-in-a-bottle."

He graciously accepted the trade and skipped back to his tent with the bottle. "Then I insist on engraving it. Just give me a few minutes and I'll have a name carved into the base for you."

I was about to decline the offer but then smiled. Engraving it would be pretty cool. But I knew Henry wouldn't want his name on display for his crew to see. "Can you very discreetly, maybe on the bottom, carve the initials H.W.W?"

"Of course, Miss," he replied. "Come, have a seat while you wait."

Now that I had a wagon, I loaded up with a few more things and when I'd finished with the market, I made my way back to The Thirsty Trout, happy with my haul and entertained ideas of all the yummy things I would make for the crew. I was still on a mission, to change Henry's mind about killing The Cobhams and then find a way back home. But who knows how long that could take? I may as well make things as comfortable as possible, make some friends, eat some delicious food.

This was the wonderful adventure I'd always dreamed of. Even as a kid, all I wanted was to sail away and live an exciting life. I thought I was doing that by moving out to Alberta, living in the big city, doing what I loved. But, truthfully, I hated my job. It was stressful and demanding, I had no real life to speak of. I had to accept the fact that the life I was living, here in the past, was far more exciting than anything I could ever dream of in the future.

I just hoped my actions last night wouldn't complicate things between Captain Barrett and I. We were both a little drunk, gave into our attraction for one another, but that's all it was. A one-time thing. So, why did I get excited at the thought of making him smile with a present? I shook my head. No, I was just trying to establish trust, be friendly. The ship-in-a-bottle was a token of that.

Then what was last night?

I sighed to myself as I entered the tavern, pulling the heavy wagon behind me. The innkeeper, whose name I'd still yet to learn, rushed over from his desk to help me.

"Well, you're an early riser, aren't ya?" he said.

"I had a list of things to get, and everyone was asleep, so I figured it best to get it done and out of the way."

"Well, you just missed them. The whole lot jumped out of their beds and ran out the door."

I nodded. "Yeah, they had some business to tend to, information to find," I replied, thinking of how Henry said they wanted to suss out the word on land regarding the Cobhams.

"They've no idea how lucky they are, those boys," he told me after checking out the things in my wagon. "You can keep this in the kitchen until you're ready to head back to your ship if you like."

"Oh, thanks, that would be great."

"And I have something for you," the old man perked up and scuttled over to the front desk where I watched him grab a stack of folded laundry.

"These are some clothes for you," he said. "They were my son's when he was a young man, I 'magine they'd fit you just fine. Much better than the linens draping off ya now."

I chuckled and glanced down at the clothes Henry had given me. They were huge, and I looked ridiculous with the bunched-up trousers held tight to my waist with my belt. Like a kid wearing their parent's clothes. I graciously accepted the bundle from him.

"Thank you so much," I said, and gave him a hug with my free arm. "Oh, I actually have something for you, too."

I pulled out a note from my pocket and handed it to him. I wrote it while I sat with the merchant and waited for him to carve Henry's initials on the bottle. "It's the recipe for the pasta dish I made last night."

The man's eyes lit up with joy and he held the piece of paper to his chest. "Well, this is better than a bag of gold shillings, Dianna."

I laughed. "Well, I'm glad you like it." I began pulling the wagon toward the kitchen. "I never did catch your name, by the way."

"Sheppard," he replied, and my breath caught at the familiar name. "Nathaniel Sheppard."

I remembered then, my mom once telling me that Dad's heritage stemmed all the way back to some of the island's first merchants and shop owners. And I wondered if Mr. Sheppard was one of them. I told myself he was, just so I could feel a sense of pride in at least one bloodline here in the past.

"Well, Nathaniel, it was an absolute pleasure to have met you," I told him and gave the man another gentle hug.

He patted me on the back and replied, "And I you, dearie."

***

After a long, glorious bath that Nathaniel's wife ran for me, I stepped into one of the outfits he gave me as a new woman. I swear, I must have shed ten pounds of dirt and grime, but it felt good to be fresh and have clothes of my own. Clothes that actually fit. Even if they were that of a teenage boy. I'd much rather the black trousers and a simple white shirt over a dress if I were to be spending my days aboard a pirate ship. The pants came with a pair of black suspenders sewed into the seams, but I actually didn't mind the look. If I were back home, I'd be a trendy hipster.

The crew still weren't back from their recon trip, so I snuck into Henry's room and placed the ship-in-a-bottle on his bedside table with a note that read *I told you I would replace it. I hope you like this one better.*

I heard the bedroom door open from behind me and I turned to find Henry standing in the doorway, breathless. I couldn't help the smile that spread across my face and I opened my mouth to speak, but he lunged across the room like a bullet and grabbed me by the arms, madness in his eyes.

"Where the Christ have you been?" he bellowed, his massive fingers digging into my flesh.

I struggled to break free, but it was useless. "I went to the market like I told you I would."

"Why didn't you take Finn?" he yelled. "Why didn't you tell someone?"

I realized then, that he'd thought I ran away. "Henry, please you're—"

His grip tightened like a vice around my limbs and I thought he'd break them. "I told you not to call me that!"

I'd had enough. I wasn't some snowflake woman that he could toss around just because he couldn't get a handle on his issues. I moved my leg back and then brought it forward in one quick thrust between his legs and sent him crumbling to the floor, coughing and gasping for air.

"Why not? It's your God damn *name*, isn't it?" I moved past him and stormed out of the room, slamming the door behind me.

In the hallway, I met Finn and I tried to hide the tears that filled my eyes. "Aye, Lassie," he said, "Where have ye been? What's the matter?"

"Just leave me alone," I told him, and he recoiled at the comment. "C-can I have your room for a while?"

He stole a glance at Henry's door, then back to me, acceptance and realization on his face, and nodded with a sigh. "I'll go fetch meself somethin' to eat."

I crawled into Finn's bed, suddenly very aware of how tired my body was. I had ignored my hangover and exhausted myself all morning. Not to mention the emotional exhaustion Henry caused me. His sudden bursts of anger and mood swings were beginning to make me dizzy and I was tired of trying so hard not to make him upset.

Suddenly, my goal of changing his mind about killing The Cobhams seemed impossible. I laid there, not sleeping, for a while, just basking in the silence when a knock came at the door and I wiped my face of tears.

"It's open," I called, thinking it was probably Finn. But I was wrong, and my eyes narrowed. "What do *you* want?"

Henry stood half in, half out of the room, his face hung in shame. "May I come in?"

I mulled it over, letting him stew for a moment. Then I sat up in bed. "Yes, if you can promise to be civilized."

He took in a deep breath and entered the room, shutting the door behind him. My chest tightened, and I curled my knees up to it. He noted my actions and I could see the ping of regret he felt. It didn't excuse it, though. My arms stung like crazy where his fingers surely left bruises.

Henry took a careful step forward, one hand behind his back. "I don't want you to be afraid of me," he started.

"Well, you have a messed-up way of showing it," I replied.

"I know," he agreed, "I have my... demons. And I need to learn to face them. But it makes me weak, angry. I'm the captain of my ship, I'm responsible and in control of my men." He paused and took another step forward. "But you..."

"You can't control me?"

Henry grinned, but it didn't hide the sadness in his black eyes. "On the contrary," he replied, "It is you who controls me."

My body began to relax, and I let go of my knees. Henry sat on the edge of the bed, careful to keep his distance.

"You turned everything upside down the second you came aboard. I locked myself in my quarters for days, stewing in a fit of wine and rage. I thought you to be some sort of ghost, or demon, come to torture me. Everything I had buried, inside, and in the damned chest, came flooding back and I was a little boy again."

My shoulders sank with pity for the damaged man before me. "Because I looked like her."

"Yes," Henry replied. "At first, I thought you were her when the men dragged your body across the deck. I was ready to kill you. I needed to before the poison of Maria's memory spread too far. But then, I snuck down to where you'd been locked up, where you slept, and I saw your face."

"What made you change your mind?"

"I told myself, once I'd escaped The Burning Ghost, that I'd never take another life if I could help it."

"But Alfred..."

"Alfred deserved to meet my pistol," Henry spat, "I never spoke a word to the crew, but he was once part of Maria's men. He confirmed as much with his last words."

My brain scrambled to remember the partial phrase he spoke that day. "May you all be met with the flame of The Burning Ghost and–"

"Never rise from the ashes," Henry finished. "It was Maria's parting words each time she'd raid and burn a vessel. I don't understand how I never knew or saw him during my time there."

I tried to remember all the painful words I'd read in Henry's journal, to consider all the horrible things he'd been through. This was a broken man who'd shut the door to his past, leaving it undealt with. No one could help him get over the trauma because he wouldn't let anyone open the door. But I'd accidentally busted through it, and I then realized that I could be the one to help him.

My hand slid across the blanket toward him, entwining my fingers with his. He stared down at our touching hands and then, to my surprise, brought them up to his lips where he placed a gentle kiss across my fingers. My heart sprang to life and my empty stomach tightened. Maybe embracing my temporary adventure could also include a little bit of romance, as long as I didn't get too attached. It seemed unavoidable at that point.

"I'll take regret to my grave over hurting you, Dianna," he spoke, "I'm so very sorry. Can you ever forgive me?"

I wanted to, I truly did. But my brain wouldn't connect with my mouth and I just sat there, silent and staring at the leather-clad pirate who sat on my bed. Then he pulled the present I'd gotten him out from behind his back and smiled.

"Where did you get this?" he asked me.

"I traded for it in the marketplace."

His head tipped back, and he took a deep breath, eyes closed. "I'd thought you were gone. I'd no idea what that would mean until I thought it actually happened. I went mad at the idea. That you'd make love to me like that, and then… leave. I felt betrayed and enraged. Gus and Finn's attempts to reel me back were futile as I stormed the streets looking for you." He took his hand back and leaned forward to rub his tired face. "And here you were, trading your own scarce belongings to get this gift for me. I'm truly the devil they say I am."

Even though I knew I shouldn't feel bad for him, my heart ached for the man. To anyone else, his actions would seem unforgivable. But not to me. I knew his secrets and I knew his past, the same as if I were part of it.

And, in a way, I was. I crawled toward him and slipped my hand through his gorgeous blonde hair. The look of surprise on his face quickly melted into a fiery yearning and he grabbed me by the waist, lifting my body with ease and setting me on his lap where his warm breath caressed my neck. I grabbed at his coat's leather collar, peeling it away as he shrugged out of it.

"You're not the devil, Henry," I told him.

Cupping my cheek, his thumb smoothed the width of my lower lip as he stared at it. "I've wanted to take this beautiful mouth the moment I heard your voice spill across it."

I leaned in and planted a slow, gentle kiss, letting him taste me. I could feel his manhood beneath my body and I swayed my hips forward, driving a deep moan from his throat.

"God, I do not deserve you," he said through clenched teeth and smoothed the hair away from my face.

"No, you don't," I replied with a grin and yanked the shirt over my head to reveal my naked breasts. "But you'll have me anyway."

CHAPTER TWELVE

What seemed like a blissful eternity later, we laid naked in Finn's bed, the warmth of the fireplace like a heavy blanket and was all that lit the room. My head rested against his shoulder and I glanced up to watch his face, mesmerized by the way the flame's shadows danced across it. Henry's fingers twirled in my curls as he stared thoughtfully at the ceiling.

"What are you thinking about?" I asked him.

"You," he replied. "I never thought I'd find a woman I could let myself be with. Not after... *her*." He paused to place a kiss on my forehead. "To be this intimate with someone, it meant opening that door, even just a little. And I couldn't fathom the idea. So, I accepted that I would forever be alone.

But then you just *appeared* one day, carrying with you all the secrets of my past."

I propped myself up, so I could see him better. "Wait, you mean..." I tried to find the right words, "Henry, have you *never* been with a woman?"

His cheeks flushed, and the fire glistened in his obsidian eyes. "Well, I mean, a scatter bar maiden, if you don't count–"

I quickly, but gently, brushed my fingers against his lips.

"No, I don't count her," I told him, saving him from speaking her name during our intimate moment. "What she did to you, that wasn't affection, that wasn't... love. It was wrong. *She's* the devil, Henry."

He shifted so he laid on his side, facing me, and took me in an embrace with his whole body; legs, arms encompassed me with desperation, as if he thought I was going to disappear, and I returned the gesture, so our naked bodies lay entwined in one another.

"Henry," I whispered against his skin, and he answered with a hum, "You can't kill her." I wanted to tell him everything, about me, how I got there, and my connection to The Cobhams.

We both moved with a heavy sigh that rolled through him and he replied, "I know."

"You do?" I confirmed with surprise and broke free from our embrace to sit up.

"Yes, I know it's what the crew expect of me, but I can't. I don't want any more blood on my hands.

Certainly not the poison that surely runs in her veins."

I saw my chance. "So, what do you plan to do?"

He shrugged. "I've no idea."

"Well, why not try and find the witch who helped you trap them in the bottle?"

If I could successfully get him on board with the idea, if we found the witch, I could help Henry trap The Cobhams and save the seas from their reign of terror. But, most of all, I hoped she could help me get back home. Magic brought me here, it was probably my only chance of getting back. I knew it was my only option but, when I looked at the man next to me, I realized he could never know. It would break him, and the plan would fall apart. I had to play along and keep Henry happy. But I knew then, how easy that would be.

Because I was falling for him. Deeper than I ever thought possible.

***

The next day, we were headed to the docks where a small boat would take us out to where The Devil's Heart was anchored and awaiting our return. Henry held my hand proudly, not caring about the whispers making their way through the crew around us.

"Have something to say, gentlemen?" he spoke loudly, daring them to speak ill of our relationship.

One of the younger boys who'd shown me kindness time and time again, Charlie, I think, stopped a few steps ahead and turned to face us.

"No, Sir," he told Henry with a proud smile, "Just nice to see ya happy, is all. Will Miss Dianna be staying with us aboard The Devil's Heart for good?"

I felt a gentle squeeze of my hand and Henry stole a glance in my direction. "That decision is Dianna's."

My throat tightened under the sudden pressure to answer, knowing that my time aboard the vessel was limited. But then I realized the double meaning behind Henry's words. The decision was mine whether I would stay aboard or not. I wasn't a prisoner. I could leave if I wanted to. But one look at his face, eagerly awaiting my answer, his coal-black eyes pleading me not to go... I couldn't think of anywhere else I'd rather be.

"For as long as you'll have me, Charlie," I assured the both of them, and I saw the instant relief of pressure melt off of Henry's chest.

"So, be sure to treat her well," he added to the deckhand.

"Aye, Captain," the boy answered happily, then tipped his cap and skipped along to join the rest of the crew.

Henry stared ahead at his men with a proud, loving look. "They're good men," he told me.

"Yeah, I'm beginning to see that."

"That Charlie, I picked him up at a port in Brighton, after spending time in London for business. The eager lad wanted to join the crew, but I turned him away, said he was too young," he paused to let out a slight chuckle, "the bugger snuck aboard, and he's never left me since. He's small, but a hard worker and just loves the sea. He… he reminds me of myself at that age."

I slipped my other hand around Henry's arm and snuggled my head against it as we casually strolled toward the water. For someone named Devil Eyes, he was a hard man to dislike. I didn't know if it had anything to do with me, but I could see the dark layers beginning to peel away from him, revealing a bright and shiny heart. If I could help him heal, to face his past and figure out the man he wants to be, then I could leave this era with no regrets.

"Captain!" someone yelled from behind us and we turned to find Finn racing down the gravel pathway. "Captain, we found them," the Scotsman said as he bent over to catch his breath.

I had no idea what he was talking about, but Henry let go of my hand and stiffened; his face alert and hardened with purpose. "Where?"

"We got word of communities on the East Coast," Finn began, "They've been raided by a man and woman, lives have been lost and they were demanding to know the whereabouts of a child, a boy, Captain."

A mixture of emotions washed over Henry's face, but I was still left in the dark. "What are you guys talking about?"

"The Cobhams," Henry told me, "They're looking for the Gaelic witch."

My stomach clenched. "What's this about a boy, then?"

"It's their son. I gave him to the witch to protect," he replied, sadly, "I wanted him to live a normal life. So, I took him, years ago. And when I found the witch to trap them in the bottle, she offered to take him. Swore she could keep him safe."

"The Cobhams had a child?" I said aloud for myself to hear it. The very thought made me sick. But... could the child be the origin of my own existence? Or had the Cobhams yet to conceive the ancestor that would create my lineage? I had no way of knowing for sure.

Henry nodded and turned to Finn. "Set a course for the community you heard about. If they're looking for the boy, then they're looking for the witch we seek. This could very well be over sooner than we'd thought."

I saw the hope on his face, the glimmer of our future Henry envisioned glistening in his eyes, and my heart ached. The sooner we found the witch, the sooner I'd be gone. I thought I'd have more time.

"Aye, Captain," Finn tipped his hat and ran off toward the docks.

We continued walking toward the water and I asked Henry, "Are you happy?"

He stopped and pulled on my arm, bringing our bodies together so he could embrace me. This pirate, this man before me, only I knew how delicate he was inside, and it killed me to think about how soon I'd be shattering what little I'd help heal.

"I'll be happier when this all ends," he told me with certainty. "Then you and I shall rule the seas with light hearts and free minds."

I couldn't answer so I kissed his soft, warm lips and laid my head against his chest. A single tear escaped the corner of my eye and I quickly wiped it away before he caught it running down my cheek.

What have I done?

CHAPTER THIRTEEN

We set sail on a trip that would last ten days, according to Finn. We'd make one stop for supplies on the South Coast and then sail straight to our destination of Cupers Cove, just slightly North of St. John's. Each day I manned my kitchen, becoming more and more comfortable in my role as ship's cook. I made simple, but delicious meals of stew, fresh bread, and their new favorite; pasta.

My swab duties were simple thanks to my unexpected helper, Charlie. It seemed he didn't care much for the tasks he did aboard the ship, as long as he was on the sea. The boy constantly radiated happiness and I became really fond of him. He told me stories of his home, back in England. The money he made aboard the ship was sent back to his mother who was ill. By what he described, it sounded like cancer, something yet to be discovered in this era, and my heart broke for the boy. I told him about my dad and we bonded over our mutual experiences.

Charlie continued to help me swab the decks, wash the tables, and even clean the lower deck where the crew slept. I braved the makeshift restroom and, with Charlie's help, constructed a better system with a bucket, sawed-off at an angle, then placed and attached over a small hole in the side of the ship. It wasn't pretty, but at least we didn't have to dump a disgusting pail of human waste each day.

On the third day, I found myself elbow-deep in dishwater as I scrubbed the pans I'd used to make breakfast. Sweet Charlie appeared, eager to help.

"Let me finish this, Miss Dianna," he told me. "You go take a break. Check in with the captain." The boy wouldn't look me in the eye when he spoke the last words and I knew then that my efforts to distance myself from Henry were too obvious.

Each evening, I would retire from my daily duties of taking care of the crew and head back to the quarters that I shared with Henry. It was easy to avoid him during the day because we both had our responsibilities aboard The Devil's Heart.

But at night...

The second our eyes laid on one another, the yearning caught fire and my efforts during the day were washed away. It almost made it worse, to distance myself from Henry for hours on end. My heart clawed at my chest from the very sight of him, begging to be near him, to touch him, and I happily crawled into bed each night to let the devil-eyed pirate ravage my body.

Today would be the first since we set sail on our mission that I'd see him in the sunlight. My pulse quickened as I neared the door to the captain's quarters, but it came to a screeching halt when I'd found that we had company. Finn and Gus stood around Henry's desk of maps while their captain paced the floors.

"G'day, lass," Finn greeted. "Is it dinner time already?"

I shook my head. "Not yet. But I do have a pot of vegetable soup simmering. Charlie's watching over it." I came and took a seat near the stern's windows, one of my favorite places on the ship. I could look out to the sea and the horizon and watch the waves.

Gus jiggled with a chuckle. "That boy's fond of ya."

"He's sweet and eager to help," I replied. "It's nice having him around. Makes my job easier." I stole a glance to Henry who stood over near his desk, wavering, as if he weren't sure I wanted him to come near. I smiled to ease his worry and I watched his body relax. Did he really care that much? About how I felt and what I thought of him? How deep had he fallen for me, I wondered, as I thought of our dwindling time together. "What are you guys doing, anyway?"

"We're trying to decide where to stop for supplies and take rest on land for a night," Henry replied.

Finn pointed to a spot on the map. "If we stop here, there's a small fishing community where we could rest and stock up on some dried cod and fresh potatoes." The Scotsman lifted an eyebrow in my direction and grinned, licking his lips under the big red beard.

I laughed. Like Charlie, Finn always made me feel happy and he adored my cooking. He saved my life when I first came aboard, and he was my friend. I'd miss him dearly when I left.

"I could make some fish and brewis," I told them, "We have a big sack of hardtack left."

Henry peered down at the spot Finn suggested and paused thoughtfully as he considered it. Then, a wicked grin flashed across his face and he looked to me as he spoke. "Yes, we shall stop there for the night. Set a course, Finnigan, we should meet landfall by dawn. And leave us, I need to speak with Dianna."

The two men nodded and left the room, shutting the door behind them. My breath caught as I watched the leather-clad pirate saunter toward me. God, he was beautiful. Like a tall, broad, and rugged angel. I'd never get used to it, and I hoped I never had to. I wanted the image of him burned into my brain, to carry it with me back to the future. To revisit it whenever I wanted to dream of the once-in-a-lifetime journey I'd had.

Henry stopped at my feet and leaned down, hovering over me as he placed two hands on the arms of my chair. "Do you wish to have an adventure, Dianna?"

The nearness of him made my head light and my heart race. His breath tickled my face. "I'm sorry, but I thought I was already having one?" I replied with a playful grin. "Sailing ships, danger," I tugged at the collar of his coat, pulling him closer so our lips brushed against one another, "a devilishly handsome pirate. What more could I ask for?"

Henry's lips moved against mine as they spread wide with a grin. He moaned, taking my mouth and engulfing me in a kiss that could surely devour me whole. I pulled away, desperate for air.

"How about treasure?" he asked, boasting a playful smirk.

"What? Are you serious? Like, real treasure? *Pirate* treasure?" The small child in me came alive and I prayed he wasn't kidding.

Henry laughed and slid his massive hands under my bottom, scooping me up. I wrapped my arms around his neck and let his little bit of facial hair tickle my skin, sending goosebumps scouring down my body.

"Of course," he answered. "What other kind of treasure is there?"

I shook my head, and replied, "I have no idea."

My legs squeezed tightly around his waist and I kissed his beautiful mouth in a slow, tender way. I let my tongue trail along the underside of his upper lip, fishing for that deep growl I longed for.

"I can think of one kind," he whispered against my face.

Those eyes, those otherworldly black holes bore into my soul, relentlessly searching for something. I wanted to protest, to tell him he had to stop. I no longer worried for his broken heart alone. The closer we grew, the more I knew my own heart was on the line and the idea of leaving Henry seemed more impossible each day. Returning home quickly became a painful desire.

"The place we're stopping at. I've been there. I stole a chest from Maria's quarters aboard The Burning Ghost. While she and Eric slept one evening, I rowed ashore and hid it in a cave."

My eyes widened. "That was very brave of you."

"Yes, well, I would have returned it to its owner, eventually. But I'd no idea where it came from." He paused thoughtfully as he carried me over to the bed and laid me down. I watched with delight as he removed his heavy leather coat and climbed in next to me. "After I trapped them in the bottle, I made it my mission to sail around and collect all the stolen goods they'd poked away. It took years. But I did it. And I returned it all to the crown, or to the families of people she'd murdered. That's how The Devil's Heart began."

"How did Finn and Gus come into the picture?" I asked and mindlessly twisted my fingers in his blonde locks.

"The age of ruthless piracy was changing, I could see it before most." His chest heaved with a long sigh and began to trail his fingertips along my arm that crossed it. "I sought out like-minded men who were growing tired of ravaging the seas and wanted a better life. Gus came first. I found him pick pocketing in Harbour Grace while waiting for a spot on a pirate crew to open. It took some convincing, I even had to share some of my experiences aboard The Burning Ghost in an attempt to sway him. It turned out, Gus had captained his own ship once and The Cobhams raided it. Killed his crew and set it ablaze. Luckily, Gus is a strong swimmer. He jumped off and swam ashore." Henry stopped to let out a slight chuckle. "Now that I think of it, I believe he's most likely the only known survivor of a Burning Ghost attack."

I moved my hand to cup his cheek and turn his head toward me. My body moved closer, and I stretched my neck to kiss him. "Aside from you."

"Huh, yes," he agreed, letting that sink in, "aside from myself."

"And Finn?"

Henry chortled. "Finn is one of the finest sailing masters I'd ever met. But no ship would have him on account of... his, uh–"

I balked at the idea. "Because of his sexual orientation?" Henry looked confused by my words and I rolled my eyes. "I mean because he prefers men?"

"Yes, that. I wasn't aware you knew. He swore me to secrecy."

I shook my head. "This era, I swear…" but caught myself before I could finish. Henry didn't seem to catch my reference to the past, so I veered the conversation back on track. "So, how did you get this big ship?"

"Ah, that was a gift from the crown for my services."

"Services? You mean as a privateer?"

I watched his eyebrows raise in surprise. "Well, you know more than you let on. And yes, you're correct." His beautiful face twisted into a devilish smirk. "In a way."

"What do you mean?"

"Word began to spread of what I was doing, sailing around on a small one-man boat to collect what I could from The Cobham's raids. The crown awarded me The Devil's Heart in exchange for continuing what I was doing, but going further and seeking out what they robbed of the Crown and other rich bureaucrats." He paused to shoot me a sly grin. "But they said nothing about raiding other pirate ships."

A gasp escaped my throat. They really were pirates, then. In a sense. "Henry!"

He hushed me and placed a hand over my mouth. "Now, now. It's not like that. We took no lives. We waited until the ships had docked and we raided them at night. We returned what we knew to have ownership and kept what didn't. It's as honest a life as a pirate could live, Dianna."

I let it sink in and realized that Henry was right. What did it hurt? He said they took no lives. They were like pirate ninjas, like the Robin Hood and the Merry Men of the sea, stealing from the bad guys and giving it back. So, I nodded in agreement and he let me go. But he seemed unsure.

"You think ill of me now?"

I examined his glorious face thoughtfully, smoothed his hair back, taking in as much of him as possible and collecting the information in my brain to paint the picture later. When I needed it. How could I think of him in any other way but fondly?

I shook my head and replied, "No. Never."

"You know more about me than any living person on this Earth, Dianna," he pointed out.

"Is that a bad thing?"

"No, I quite like it, actually," he assured me and planted a warm kiss to my forehead. "But I know nothing of you. Tell me."

Panic set in. What could I possibly tell him that would even make sense? "What do you want to know?"

"Anything. Everything."

My mind flipped through memories of my life like a picture book, trying to figure out what to say and how to say it. "Well, my mother—"

"What was her name?"

"Constance," I answered, careful not to say her last name. "She came to Newfoundland and met my dad, Arthur Sheppard, and fell in love. She was a baker and taught my dad everything she knew. They opened a bakery and then had me, they taught me everything, hoping I'd one day take it over."

"And you didn't?"

"I was a dreamer, I guess you could say?" I laughed at the thought. "I convinced myself there was more out there in the world for me than to stay home in our tiny, small-minded community and be a baker."

"And what happened then?" Henry had rolled to his side to face me, propping his head up on one arm, enthralled in the words I had to say.

"She died," I replied with barely a whisper. I single tear escaped my eye and Henry's thumb reached out to catch it as it rolled down my cheek. "She... drowned at sea. When I was a teenager. I had been considering staying home for a few years to help with the bakery, but after she was lost, when we never found her body, my father sort of lost his mind. Went mad with grief. I felt so alone so I... ran away. Became a cook for rich people."

To my surprise, Henry replied, "I can imagine what he felt."

"Because you went through it with your parents?"

"Well, yes, in a way. I cried for months over their deaths, but I was trapped in a void of constant fear,

I'm not sure I ever properly grieved for them." The man next to me leaned in and pressed his body to mine. "But the thought of losing you…"

I told myself I would refrain from letting things get deeper, but I couldn't help it, Captain Barrett had my heart in his hands and could so easily mold it to his will. I let a slight whisper escape my lips, "I know."

"It would end me."

I only nodded in reply and Henry grabbed my head, holding it to his chest where I happily remained, comfortable and satisfied in his warm embrace. We talked for hours, discovering one another in a whole new way. Then, we eventually drifted off to a world where I knew we both could live, in our dreams.

Together.

CHAPTER FOURTEEN

The next day we met landfall near the small community we planned to stop at for the night. After we checked in at a tavern, I found myself in the room Henry and I was sharing. I wanted to rest, but he held out my jacket and smiled.

"Are you ready?" he asked and then looked to the clock in the corner of the room. "We don't have much time."

"What, is there a time limit to when the treasure is available?" I asked sarcastically and grabbed my coat from his arms, slinging it over my shoulders. I no longer thought of it as Maria's. This jacket came back through time with me, kept my skin from burning in the sun while I clung to that chest and bobbed in the sea, and it's kept me warm on cold nights aboard the ship. It was every bit mine.

"As a matter of fact, there is," he replied with all seriousness.

We skipped down the stairs like two children eager for an adventure, with no worries in the world. Finn approached us before we got to the door.

"Where're the two of ye headed off to?"

"We have something to tend to, Finnigan," Henry replied, and I tried to hide my grin at the use of Finn's full name. I could tell it bothered him by the slight twitch his face gave, but not enough to say anything when his captain used it. "Mind the men and take Gus to suss out the word on land. See if you can find some new information about The Cobhams."

Finn nodded. "Aye, Captain." Then he shot me a look I knew I was going to miss. The kind an older brother would give his kid sister when he wanted to tease her but couldn't in front of the parents. "Milady."

"I brought some fresh rosemary buns with me. I put some on your bed," I told him.

He lit up before hopping away and bounded up the stairs, his long legs easily taking three at a time. I was going to miss him dearly.

***

Henry led the way as we scaled the rocky shore near the small community. The sun shone down from high in the sky, and it sparkled on the ocean like wet crystals.

"How much further?" I asked him.

"Not far," he replied and reached back to take my hand. Not that I needed it. Growing up in a coastal community meant that I spent the majority of my early days playing down by the water, hopping across rocks, building rafts, jigging for squid with nothing but a stick and some line. I loved the sea and everything that came with it. But I let him be chivalrous.

Any sign of life was far out of sight as we approached the mouth of a cave, nestled away in the rocky walls of the cliffs above. I felt like I walked into a storybook, full of wonder and fantasy as we entered, and the sounds of the waves turned into echoes around us.

"Is it in here?" I asked.

"Yes, but we've a way to go yet," he vaguely replied. "Here."

Henry stopped and stared down at a hole in the floor of the small cave, barely large enough for us to fit in. It reminded me of a manhole. I peered in and saw that it was full of water. The water emitted an aqua glow that illuminated the granite around us like strange, magical twinkle lights.

"Down *there*?" I asked, my voice cracking.

Henry picked up a rock, about the size of a basketball, and handed it to me. I nearly dropped it, the weight pulling me down, and he picked up another similar one for himself.

"When I first found this cave, I was holding the small chest in my arms. I had no idea this blowhole was here, and it was dark. I fell into it and would have surely drowned. The opening was so deep and narrow with nothing to hold on to. But, thankfully I held the chest and it caused me to sink to the bottom." He shifted his stance and grasped the rock tightly. "These rocks should do."

I shook my head in confusion. "Wait, you want me to hold this rock and jump into that tiny hole?" His answer was a cheeky smirk. "No, no way in Hell am I doing that. You can go. I'll wait here."

"Dianna, look at me." I tore my eyes from the hole at my feet and gazed up at Henry. "I would never put you in danger. Do you trust that?"

I stared at him, searching for a sign, any waver in his certainty, but found none. This is what I wanted, wasn't it? A grand adventure and someone to share it with? I sucked in a deep breath and clutched the rock to my chest.

"Fine, let's do it. Quickly, before I change my mind."

Henry beamed. "I'll go first. Just hold the rock tightly and let yourself sink. Don't fight it. I'll see you on the other side."

I watched in terror as Henry pencil-dove into the narrow hole and saw his head quickly fade away. I panicked, my heart racing, and I couldn't bring myself to do it. But then, I heard my mother's voice whispering softly in my ear and I closed my eyes to better hear the sweet sound.

"*Never turn your back on an adventure, Dianna, baby*," the voice told me, and I swore I felt her delicate hand on my shoulder. *"Most people are too blind to see,"* her face brushed my hair as it neared my ear, *"open your eyes, baby."*

My tear-filled eyes flew open and I grasped the rock tight before jumping into the hole, feet and heart first. I held my breath as my body rapidly sunk to the never-ending bottom. My lungs tingled as they began to run out of air and I wondered if I went too far, maybe I was supposed to lean a certain way or something.

But my feet touched the soft, sandy bottom and I saw a glow coming from the right, where the narrow hole seemed to veer off into an L-shape. I dropped the rock and bent my knees, launching myself toward the light. Something grabbed a hold of my arm and yanked hard, pulling me up and out of the water where I gasped and clawed for air.

"Oh, my God!" I cried out, lungs still burning from air deprivation. Henry helped me to my feet and wrapped his arms around my drenched body. "That was insane!"

I saw the carefree smile he wore, it was the happiest I'd ever seen him; as if the rush of adrenaline pumped life back into his stiff body and I couldn't help but laugh. He joined in and the sound our laughter echoed off the cavern walls around us.

Our wet faces came together in a passionate kiss, the taste of saltwater mixing with the sweet flavor of Henry's lips and I delighted in it, taking in as much as I could as if I were starving for him. I felt him pull away and he gazed into my adrenaline-crazed eyes.

"I love you, Dianna."

Everything in my body came to a screeching halt, my ears filled with the sound of my heavy pulse, and I just stared at the man before me, mouth gaping but empty of sound.

The pirate shook his head and smoothed the soaked curls away from my face. "It's okay, you don't have to say anything. I know it's unexpected. I just," his chest heaved with the intake of a deep breath, "I just had to say it. I know it's only been a short while that we've known each other but I carried the words in my mouth for days now, and I wanted you to have them."

My mouth still hung open as my brain searched for a response. "Henry, I—"

As if sensing my hesitation, Henry took me by the hand and broke free of our embrace. "It was right over here that I hid it," he told me, the sound of his voice echoing off the cavern walls that covered us.

As we headed to the rocky side of the cavern, I searched around to take in my surroundings. We were completely underground. What I thought to be a blowhole was some sort of tunnel that led to an underground cave, bigger than the one we first entered. A mound of rock occupied the center of where we stood, and a small moat of water surrounded the perimeter.

Then, I watched as Henry, ankle-deep in water, forcefully removed stones from a spot in the wall.

They fell and crumbled at our feet as he dug deeper and deeper. Finally, he pulled something from the cavity and let the weight of it fall to the ground. It was a chest, almost an exact match to the one that started my journey to the past.

"Holy crap," I whispered to myself. Now, *this* was a real-life pirate's chest.

Henry fished a ring of keys from his pocket and seemed to know exactly which one to use as he expertly flipped to it and then opened the brass lock. The lid creaked open to reveal a half-full chest of gold coins, trinkets, jewels, and other otherworldly treasures. My eyes widened with fascination and I kneeled next to Henry.

"This is ours, Dianna," he told me, "after this is all over, we can use this to start a new life together. If you would want."

I couldn't bring myself to look him in the eye. This man from another time confessed his love for me. Henry saw a future for us that would never happen. And I would be the one to take it all away from him. I realized then, I had to tell him. But, when I finally brought my eyes to meet his hopeful gaze, I decided to wait until later that night. For now, I wanted to have our adventure. That much I could give him.

I stuck my hand in the chest, letting my fingers swim through the cold, wet contents with amazement. "These things are miraculous. I feel bad keeping any of it."

Henry fished out a long gold chain and looped it over my head. I looked down at the heavy egg-shaped ruby that hung from it.

"Oh, no, I could never–"

"It's yours," he insisted. "Along with everything else in here. Accept that, Dianna. We'll live like kings and queens."

I felt a twinge of pain in my chest from his words. It felt as if Henry was falling deeper and deeper in love with me, at a rate I couldn't keep up with. I should have told him before this, I should have told him last night when we laid in bed, divulging all the tiny details of our lives to one another.

I wondered how he would react when I told him; when I'd surely crush his heart, stripping away the little I helped to heal. Would he kill me? Did I think he was capable of that? Maybe he'd hold me prisoner and return me to that storage cell on deck. My aunt once said that the mind of a dying man is a lonely place. And I wondered, then, how the mind of a heart-broken man looked.

I could tell Henry sensed my emotions, but he chose to ignore it, shutting the chest and rising to his feet. "Right, very well," he said. I stood to meet him and tucked the necklace inside my shirt. "Let's head back, shall we?"

I couldn't believe it took me that long to realize, I'd been so enthralled in our adventure, but how were we supposed to get out? We couldn't go back the way we came, gravity just didn't work like that. I craned my neck and searched around, my eyes landing on the source of light which filled the cavern.

"Wait," I spoke and narrowed my eyes at Henry who sported a playful smirk. "Are you kidding me?" There, just a few feet above the floor of the cavern was a hole filled with light. "Why didn't we just come in that way?"

Henry shrugged and bent down to pick up the heavy chest. "Now, where would be the fun in that?"

CHAPTER FIFTEEN

We arrived back at the tavern just in time for supper. I'd been silent the whole way home, my mind racing with all the different scenarios of how I could tell Henry my secret. None of them ended well. I made myself sick with worry and could barely get down more than a few bites of the moose stew the inn's cook served us. Thankfully, Henry's attention was held by Finn and Gus who had been spewing the details of their day. They heard more whispers of The Cobhams ravaging the East Coast. It seemed they were hanging around one main area, so we were still on track to find them and the Gaelic witch.

And my ticket home.

I ascended the stairs to the rooms above as Henry held my hand and led the way. I was so engulfed in my cloud of shame and worry that I hadn't noticed that he acted strangely. Like he was nervous about something. Maybe it was from talking about The Cobhams and knowing how close we were to them. He'd have to face some old demons real soon, and I knew how hard that must be for him to imagine.

We entered our room and I turned to close the door behind me. When I spun back around, I found Henry down on one knee, and a tiny object held in his one hand. The candlelight glistened off a large emerald stone that sat within a gold claw, its thick loop pinched between Henry's fingers.

My breath caught in my throat, all form of words or thoughts fleeing from my brain. This was not the way I expected the evening to go. But, still, my heart yearned for the words to spill from his mouth, the ultimate declaration of love, and I chastised myself for wanting it.

"Dianna," he said, mouth trembling, "I wanted to ask you today in the cave, but I had to be sure this ring was still inside. It was my mother's–"

I stepped closer. "Oh, Henry…"

"Maria stole it from my home and I took it back when I left her ship that night. I swore to keep it safe and return for it when I was ready." He paused, and I watched his face glow with excitement. "I'm ready. I want to share my life with you, the life you've given back to me. Dianna, will you marry me?"

Tears spilled over the edge of my eyes and I hid my face in shame. Finally, I shook my head. "Henry, I'm so sorry…"

He stood and came to me, prying my hands away from my face. "What's wrong?"

"I-I can't marry you."

I may as well have driven a knife through the man's heart for the pain I witnessed enter his body. He fell back a step and clutched his chest.

"What do you mean? What are you saying?" And then a whisper, "You can't care for me?"

"No, I do," I assured him, noting his use of the word *can't* rather than *don't*, as if he truly believed himself unlovable. "I really do, Henry, I swear. So much, you have no idea." My trembling hand reached up to wipe my face. "But that's what makes this so hard."

His face twisted with emotions and he fought with my words. "What did I do? Was it because… I hurt you?"

"Oh, God, Henry, no," I told the man and stepped toward him. "I showed up here and ended up on your ship. I never expected to live through the first day, let alone make it to now. Or to have fallen for you this way. This fast."

I watched his face harden as he fought back tears. "Then what is it? Another man? Are you betrothed to someone else?"

"No, it's not another man. It's another place."

He recoiled, confusion flooding his expression and I urged myself to continue, to make him understand. Rip the band-aid off.

"Henry, I'm not from this time."

"I don't understand."

"I was born in the twentieth century," I began, "and I came here from the year two thousand eighteen. My mother collected things from the past. Artifacts. Your chest, for one. After my father's death a couple of weeks ago, I returned to my childhood home to settle things. I found your chest among my mother's stuff and opened it. I accidentally broke the ship-in-a-bottle and a massive wave came crashing in through my house, sweeping me away. I woke up, clutching the chest, and that's when Finn and Gus pulled me from the water. I feared for my life when I discovered who your enemy was… because my name is Dianna Cobham. Maria is my… ancestor."

I stopped to catch my breath and to let the words sink into him, which didn't seem to be doing very well. Henry's head shook as he fought with my terms, rejecting them. The man refused to respond, and his body vibrated with anger.

"I wanted you to find the witch, so I could save my lineage and then ask for her help to send me back. And, well, you know the rest."

Silence filled the room and Henry turned, walking toward the window where he stopped and hung his head. His silence was killing me, so I closed the distance between us and braved to touch his shoulder. He reacted with a swift turn, knocking me down on the floor, and his sword unsheathed.

"You lie!"

My eyes widened in panic at the sharp tip, just inches from my face. "H-Henry, no, I swear!"

The blade pressed against my chest and his eyes gleamed with madness. "Then you *used* me, played me for a fool!"

I couldn't think of a proper response because, from his side, I could see why he would think that. And, in a way, I did. But I never deliberately leveraged his feelings for me. I would have gladly sought another way if I could have. But, like him, I was weak and gave in to my emotions.

Henry's breathing quickened to borderline hyperventilating, madness and betrayal toiling in his eyes. He squeezed them shut, seemingly fighting with himself, and retracted the blade. "Get out."

"Henry, please, just list—"

"Don't ever call me that again! Get out!"

I scrambled to my feet as he swung the sword in my direction, and ran out of the room, my feet barely touching the floor as I descended the stairs to a quiet and empty tavern below. I found a corner with a large armchair and curled up in it where I laid awake for hours, crying silently to myself, before exhaustion set in and I finally fell asleep. I took one thought with me as I plunged into a dream.

I'd broken him.

***

We boarded The Devil's Heart bright and early the next day. Henry wouldn't come within ten feet of me, so I took my place next to Finn and helped him load the supplies. He looked possessed, like a zombie, unable to make eye contact with anyone. For two days, I watched as he moved from place to place, ordering the crew with pointing, grunting, and glaring. The atmosphere aboard the ship turned cold and silent, unlike the homey feel I suddenly realized I'd come to love.

Finn gladly accepted me back into his double hammock; said I was like a small, warm teddy bear. My duties never ceased, though. I cooked three square meals a day for the crew, *my* crew, the men and boys I adored. They loved me, too, I knew that. But they realized I'd made their captain fall into a strange pit of despair, and I felt their unease around me. Especially old man Maurice. He watched me from where he sat each day, his beady eyes examining my every move. He was the only crew member I'd yet to come to know well, and his constant leering made me uneasy.

With less than three days left to our journey, I began to grow restless. I didn't want to leave this era without reconciling with Henry if only a little. I just couldn't stand the thought of his hatred for me living on throughout history. Who knows how much I'd already changed the course of the history that I knew? I could find myself in an unknown world when I finally returned. Or maybe not at all. Perhaps I'd simply put everything back on course, returning Henry to the cold and ruthless pirate he was before my arrival.

I had planned to say my goodbyes to Finn, Gus, and Charlie before the rest of the crew. They'd come to be like family to me. Brothers. But, first, I wanted to try Henry. The man hardly left his quarters. I made a tray of food each day and tasked young Charlie with bringing it to him. But that morning I'd made toutans, Henry's favorite, as a peace offering of sorts.

"I'll bring this to the captain, milady," Charlie said as he reached for the tray.

"That won't be necessary," I told him, "I'll bring it."

His eyes widened. "Are you sure? I don't mind."

I gave the sweet boy a smile. God, I was going to miss him. He was like the little brother I never had. "No, I'll be fine. Can you stay here and make sure the men get theirs? And be sure to grab some for yourself? I made plenty extra, so fill your belly."

I could tell he didn't want to hand over the task, so loyal to his captain. But the child inside took over and he happily accepted my place behind the counter. I'd shown him enough and hoped he would take over for me as ship's cook when after I left. I removed my apron and headed to Henry's quarters with the tray of toutans and fresh molasses. I knocked on the door but got no response, so I pushed it open and entered quietly.

The smell was atrocious, and I held my breath as I carried the tray to his desk. No candles were lit, and the drapes had been partially closed over the large stern windows, casting the room in a dreary grey.

Then I spotted a figure sitting in a chair, his face cast out to the ocean behind us where the drapes pulled back slightly. The only movement I found was the slow rise and fall of his chest.

"Hen–" I stopped myself, determined not to anger him, "Captain Barrett. I brought you some food."

My fingers fiddled at my sides as I fought for words. Something caught my eye on the table next to Henry and my heart sank when I realized it was a pile of dishes, still full of food, days old. He wasn't eating.

"Look, my time is coming to an end here. When we find the Gaelic witch, I'll be gone, and you can move on with your life. I just… I just couldn't stand the thought of leaving things like this. I want you to know… that I do care for you. More than I ever thought possible. It was never my intention to hurt your feelings. You captured my heart before I could figure out a way home, and then things just worked out the way they did. I just wanted to be honest with you."

He didn't flinch, let alone respond. It was as if I weren't even in the room. The man was like a ghost. Then again, I didn't belong there, and my stomach clenched as I realized… I was the ghost. I turned to leave but stopped at the door and glanced back.

"You're so good, Henry," his name elicited a slight sigh, "It only took a moment for me to see it and, when I did, it captivated me. Please don't forget that, don't let go of your heart."

***

The sun was setting on the horizon and I leaned against the side of the ship, taking it in. I'd watched hundreds of sunsets but none like this, out there on the open water. Calm, soothing waves lapped at the side of the boat while the orange and purple glow of the sun slowly faded into the distance, leaving behind a trail of darkness.

I watched the transformation and relished the beauty of witnessing the ancient sun falling asleep, the moon taking its place to play with the waves. It was an image I filed away in my mind, to revisit in the future when I needed another reminder of the grand adventure I had.

The tired men had gone below, leaving me behind on the quiet deck. Finn approached me before heading down for himself.

"Aye, lassie," he said quietly and grabbed hold of my shoulders to squeeze me in his crushing embrace. I'd come to expect it now. Enjoy it, even. "Are ye comin' to bed?"

I wrapped my red jacket tightly across my chest and took in the sweet smell of the midnight ocean.

"Not yet," I replied. "I like it up here this time of night. I can think."

He rubbed his big red beard, unsure of what to do. "Look, I ain't no fool, lass," he told me, "We all ken ye and the captain are fond of each other. Whatever happened, I'm sure ye can forgive him, no?"

I was surprised to learn that Finn assumed Henry had done something to hurt me, to push me away. When, really, it was me who'd messed everything up. "Thanks, Finn, but you're wrong. Captain Barrett–" I struggled for words. There was no way to make him understand. "I betrayed his trust. I didn't mean to, but I did, and he may never forgive me." My body turned, and I took the Scotsman's freckled hands in mine. "You have to promise me something."

"Of course," he replied and stood a little straighter, prouder. "Anythin' for ye."

Tears welled in my eyes. Not in a million years would I have ever dreamed of such goodness in one man. He lived in a time not worthy of his heart. "I need you to take care of Henry. Make sure he doesn't fall into darkness. He's going to be facing some demons when we hit land; when we find The Cobhams, and he's going to need all the help he can get."

Finn shrugged, still unclear on what I was asking. "Well, yes, I'd lay down me life for the captain in a battle."

I shook my head. "No, not just physically. He's going to need you afterward. You and Gus. Be his family. Don't let him lose sight of his heart. He's finally figured out how to use it again."

The man let out a puff of air and chuckled. "Christ, ye sound like a damn tragic fairy tale."

I laughed, what little I could with the weight of a broken heart in my chest. "Oh, and I never said thank you."

"Fer what?"

"Saving my life when I first came aboard."

He chortled. "Yeah, well, a good lot that did. Yer leavin' me anyway."

I felt my heart sink. He was right. Finn was no damn fool. He knew I was leaving. I didn't know what to say so I just let the cool silence of the night air fill the space between us.

"Do ye want me to stay up here with ye?"

I managed a smile for my friend and shook my head. "No, go to bed. I'm going to sit up here and watch the stars."

I laid down on a large crate and listened to the sound of Finn's steps retreating to the deck below until the waves, the creaking of the ship, and my own breaths were the only sounds to be heard. My fingers reached up to clasp around the large pendant of the necklace Henry had given me and cringed as the images of his pained expression flashed through my mind. I'd never broken anyone's heart before and the guilt was something I'd carry with me forever. I wish I had time to fix things, to piece together the shards of his shattered heart. Then a strange and unexpected thought dawned on me.

Why did I still want to go back home?

I had nothing waiting for me back there. No boyfriend, no friends, definitely no job. Maybe I could talk to the witch, find a way home but not use it yet. What kind of person would I be if I just left Henry in the past after I'd crushed him like that?

At some point, I'd drifted off, lulled by the soothing rock of The Devil's Heart. I knew I was dreaming for the fact that Henry was with me. He laid me down on the same sandy beach I dreamed of before, and his able hands caressed my body. I felt his fingers fumble with the buttons of my shirt, unable to get them undone. I let out a giggle and tried to look at his face but all I saw was a black figure, silhouetted by the blaring sun behind it. His hands grew impatient and began tugging hard.

My heart sped up as the bright sun disappeared and all that remained was darkness. Panic forced me from my dream and my eyes fluttered open to find someone was actually tearing at my shirt. I opened my mouth to scream but a salty hand cupped it and pushed me back down. I struggled against the heavy figure and my knee caught him in the head, turning his face toward me where the moonlight revealed my attacker.

Maurice.

The old pirate was trying to rape me and had my body pinned to the crate underneath.

"Now that the captain is done with ya, I figures I'll have a go."

His raunchy breath blanketed my face and it took all I had not to vomit. My naked breasts chaffed under the rough terrain of his jacket and I felt him shift as he fetched something from his pocket.

The sound of a blade sliding from its sheath set me over the edge and I flew into panic mode. With only one of his arms holding me down, I managed to twist my head enough to uncover my mouth and I let out a scream. It was stopped short, though, when Maurice threw a blow to my jaw. My ears rang, and my head swam as it threatened to black out. His blade rested between my legs where I felt the quick thrust of it slicing into the crotch of my trousers.

Maurice's entire body held me down, and I succumbed to the weight of it, my lungs hardly able to take in a breath. Tears poured from my eyes as I accepted what was happening. But before I gave up entirely, the man's heavy figure ripped from my body and I glanced up to find Henry standing over me.

"Maurice!" he bellowed, a pistol aimed straight ahead. "How dare you put your hands on her!"

The man brought himself to his knees. "Captain, I beg of you, I had no idea. I thought you were—"

Henry lunged forward and put the clunky pistol to Maurice's forehead. "Were *what*? Done with her?

You disgust me. I should end your life right here, right now." I could see the shakiness in his arm, in the way he held the gun. I stood and placed my hand on Henry's arm, and he turned to look at me, his eyes enraged and full of tears. "He deserves to die, Dianna."

"Yes, but you don't deserve to kill him," I replied. Henry shouldn't bear the burden, shouldn't have the blood on his hands. I knew how much it hurt him. "Tie him up. We'll have him arrested when we meet landfall." The pistol never wavered from the direction it pointed, and I tightened my grip around his arm. "*Henry*."

I watched as the heaviness of rage left Henry's body and he handed me the gun. Then, as if it killed him to stand there and not touch me, his desperate hands took my face and pressed it to his chest where I could hear his heart beating wildly.

"God, I heard you scream and it was as if someone had shot me through the chest."

I didn't answer, I just let him hold me and breathed in as much of him as I could. Just a few days apart had now felt like an eternity and I realized something. Perhaps, I knew it all along but didn't want to accept it because we'd only known each other a short while, or maybe for fear it would prevent me from going home.

I loved him.

I was about to speak the words when I caught a glimpse of movement in the corner of my eye. Maurice had lunged for the pistol I set down on the crate and my body took on a mind of its own. I wrapped my fingers around the hilt of Henry's sword and yanked it from his side. It all happened so fast, *too* fast, but I didn't want this man's blood on Henry's soul. I swung the heavy blade to the side and heaved it back toward Maurice where it sliced through his body and came to a stop in the center of his chest.

"Dianna!" Henry yelled next to me.

He tried to pry the sword from my grasp, but my hands had a death grip around the hilt. My mind was screaming for me to let go, but I couldn't. I could only stare at the man whose life was dissolving before my eyes, the life I took, his wide gaze looking up at me as the blood drained from his carcass and began running toward my feet. Just then, footsteps came hurdling in our direction.

"Captain!" Finn called, "What the Christ is going on here?"

"I found Maurice attempting to force himself on Dianna," Henry replied. "I made my orders quite clear on that."

"Aye," Gus answered and let out a long breath, "Did she—"

"Yes, before I had the chance," Henry told them and ripped my shaking hands away before sweeping me into his arms. I felt him pull my jacket closed, covering my naked breasts and he kissed my forehead. "Can you take care of this?"

"Aye, Captain," Finn responded dutifully.

Henry began walking, taking me away from the scene. "Christ, Dianna, what were you thinking?"

"Uh, better me than you?" I offered a weak and shaky response.

We entered his quarters and the warmth of the fireplace began to thaw my chilled skin. I didn't even realize I was cold until then. My mind slowed and the reality of what I'd done started to smooth out. Maurice was going to rape me. Then, who knows what else? I was strong. I could live with it, deal with it. I could even get some professional help when I got back home if I needed to.

But, the old man was going to kill Henry, and the captain would have surely taken his life. I couldn't let him live with it. For *that* to be one of his memories of me. The woman he damned himself to save, only to have lost her. No, I would carry that burden for him.

Henry paced the floor in front of me. "I've enough blood on my hands, Dianna. What's one more drop? Now you have to live with *this*."

"I did it for you," I told him.

"For me?" he chortled, still pacing. "You did this for *me*? Why would–" He came to a halt, his eyes locking on mine. They sparkled with a glimmer of hope. "Why?"

Even though I admitted it to myself, I still couldn't form the words for him. My shoulders gave a shrug. "I just... I didn't want you to do it. I knew it would eat you up inside."

"No," he replied curtly.

"No?"

"Tell me why, Dianna." The devil-eyed pirate sauntered toward me and came to a stop at my feet, our chests touched and moved together in unison with each quick breath.

The nearness of him never ceased to make me weak, influencing my mind and body. And my heart. "You know why," I whispered.

Henry pinched my chin between his finger and thumb, forcing my gaze upward. "I want to hear you say the words. I deserve as much, do I not?"

The deep rasp in his voice was like hot wax melting down my center. "Because… I love you." I felt the breath catch in his chest as the pirate took my mouth in desperation, the sorrow he carried giving way and making room for me again. I was where I was meant to be, there, in Henry's arms. I never wanted him to let me go. Then an idea came to life in my mind and I laughed to myself for not considering it before.

"Henry," I managed to speak. Our mouths still entwined. He moaned a response and refused to stop kissing me. "Come with me."

Everything slowed, and he broke free from our embrace. "What? To the future?" He spoke the words, but I could tell he didn't believe them.

"Yes, come back. Be with me," I pleaded. The more I thought about it, the more it made sense. I pulled out the snow globe key chain again and handed it to him. "We could live together in my home by the ocean. I could run my parent's bakery. It's beautiful and quiet, you could fish every day."

I could see him contemplating it as he examined the tiny, foreign object. I saw, then, the yearning in his eyes for the life he once wanted. "What would I do there? What about my crew?" Henry shook his head and began to walk away. "Dianna, I don't belong three hundred years in the future. I have no grasp of what that even means."

My hand took his and pulled him back to me. "You belong with me. Wherever that might take us." I placed a gentle kiss on his mouth. "And you told me once, Gus was a captain, right? Couldn't he captain The Devil's Heart in your place?" He wouldn't respond, only stared off into a void above my head. And then my guts turned heavy at a thought. "I mean, unless you don't want to be with me anymore."

Henry snapped out of his daze and his black eyes pierced my heart. "Christ, Dianna, there's nothing in this world I want more. I crave you more than I desire to breathe, to eat, even. Nothing I'd experienced aboard The Burning Ghost came close to preparing me for the torment I've endured the last few days."

His glorious mouth, the words that spilled from it, and the delicious scent of him pulled me in like a siren's call. My breathing quickened, and hot goosebumps scoured my body at the very thought of having him. I removed my jacket and let it fall to the floor, my partially exposed breasts heaving and inviting him to take me.

"No," he said to my surprise, "I can't. I won't. Not after..."

Did he see me as tainted? Now that my body had been violated? Or now that he knew Maria's blood ran in my veins. I recoiled at the thought. "Y-you don't want me?"

Henry grabbed a quilted blanket from the bed and came to wrap it around my shoulders before scooping me into his arms, something he always seemed to do with ease.

"I will always want you, Time Traveller." I mirrored his grin at the endearing nickname. "And I shall. Soon. But not tonight." He laid me down on the bed and wrapped the blanket tight. "No, tonight, I'll take comfort in knowing you're safe and in my arms."

And that's exactly where I remained.

CHAPTER SIXTEEN

The Devil's Heart anchored just off the shore of the small coastal community of Cuper's Cove. I laid in bed that morning, with the velvet curtains closing me in, while I listened to Henry, Gus, and Finn discuss where to stop.

"We don't want word to spread that we've arrived," Gus pointed out.

"There's an inlet right 'ere," Finn jumped in, "It's not on the map. But I know it's there, I've seen it with me own eyes. We could drop anchor, remain hidden, and come in over the hills here."

"Right, then," Henry agreed, and I heard the shuffle of maps being rolled around, "We meet landfall in two hours. Go, ready the ship."

A couple of hours later, I found myself leaving behind our rowboats and hiking the small foothills behind Cuper's Cove and quickly realized where we were. I stopped and stood, placing my hand over my brow to block out the blazing sun above.

"This is Cupids," I said to Henry who walked next to me. He hadn't let me leave his sight since the night before.

"What do you mean?" he asked.

"This place," I continued but lowered my voice so only he could hear, "I know it. It's called Cupids where I come from. We all know it as the very first British settlement on the North American continent. It's the first English and Irish colony in Newfoundland. Like, ever. It would totally make sense for a Gaelic witch to be hiding here. She's probably with her people."

Henry smiled, taking it all in. "I never realized how strange you speak sometimes." Then he took my hand in his. "But I wager we're in the right place, then, Time Traveler. Shall we?"

We decided to split up into two groups, to scour the area better and faster. Finn, Gus, and Charlie— who'd insisted on coming against Henry's orders— and then Henry and I. Before we went our separate ways, I felt compelled to say something to Charlie.

I cupped his sweet child-like face in one of my hands. "Now, please, be careful. Don't do anything stupid. Don't be a hero." He looked confused at the last request. "Just... be invisible. Find out whatever information you can and then head back to the boats. Okay?"

He nodded. "Yes, milady." Then the boy shot Henry a brave look. "Don't let anything happen to Dianna."

Henry fought back a grin and feigned a look of offense. "Never, my good man. You can be sure the lady is in good hands."

I watched as Charlie skipped off to join his group.

"Finn is correct," Henry spoke, "The boy adores you."

I smirked. "Jealous?" Henry only laughed in good sport. "He's sweet, and probably one of your most loyal men. I think he could easily take my place as the ship's cook. I've taught him everything I know."

The man's grip tightened around my fingers. "Then be sure to tell Gus," he paused and waited for me to look at him, "it'll be up to him."

I could hardly hold back the excitement I felt. "Wait, does that mean—"

The leather-clad pirate took me by the waist and crushed his body against mine, pressing our foreheads together. "I'd follow you to the ends of the universe, Time Traveler. I belong to you."

I could have stayed there on the hilltop with him all day, celebrating the good news, but we had more important things to tend to.

"Come on, let's go catch us a witch."

***

Cuper's Cove was a merchant settlement for all sorts of ships to trade goods across the Atlantic. We entered the marketplace full of merchant and traders the scent of dried fish, spices, and other things I couldn't name hung heavy in the air. I zipped through the thick crowds of people, casting glances at tables, inside tents, searching for any sign of… something. Anything. We had no idea what we were looking for, specifically, but a Gaelic witch would surely leave some sort of trail to follow, wouldn't she?

"How did you find her before?" I whispered to Henry.

"I didn't mean to," he told me, "I was over near Harbour Grace with their son in tow; running, hiding, terrified that Maria would find us. I hadn't escaped her ship for more than a few weeks, but the fear of discovery nearly killed me. I contemplated going back to her, to trade the stress for something more familiar. The boy was no more than a few years old and I had no idea how to care for him." We emerged at the end of the market, leaving the bustling merchant and traders behind us. "The witch came to me. Offered a way to stop The Cobhams if I would help. I agreed, and the boy remained with her, with the Gaelic people. Hidden and safe."

I chewed at my bottom lip. "Well, that really tells us nothing." I worried that we'd never find the witch. The Cobhams would run free and I'd never get back home. "Maybe we should go meet up with the crew? See if they found anything?"

Henry heaved a sigh. "I suppose that's all there is to do at the moment," he looked up at the sky. "The sun will be going down soon."

We began our long hike back to the hilltops, walking in silence. I wondered what he was thinking about but never dared ask. I was eager to complete our mission and return home. Such a simple, straightforward means to an end for me. But Henry's whole world was soon going to change to something completely unknown to him. I opened my mouth to speak but something caught my eye in the forest we walked alongside.

I grabbed his arm and whispered, "Henry, look. What is that?"

We stopped and stared into the forest, the setting sun stealing the light and leaving behind darkness to flood it. At first, I thought I saw a small fire burning, but the flame appeared to be a blueish-green and jumped from side to side, taunting us.

"Well, I'll be damned," Henry spoke and moved toward the flame in awe. "It's a wil-o-the-wisp."

I held back. "A what?"

"Wil-o-the-wisp," he said again, delight smeared across his face, "They light the way for lost travellers. I've never seen one, I thought them to be a myth." His grin spread wider and he willed me to make the connection. "A *Gaelic* myth."

My pulse raced, and I stumbled over the marsh, following Henry into the dark forest, the tiny green flame dancing through the air as it led the way. We trailed behind it for at least half an hour, struggling to keep up. Over roots, under branches, and across narrow creeks, I kept my eyes on the anomaly. Mesmerized by the otherworldly creature before me.

I wanted to get a better look at it, but the closer I got, the further it danced away from us. But, suddenly, we stopped, and Henry held out his arm before me, guarding my body. The wil-o-the-wisp came toward us and I could feel Henry tense. But I wasn't scared, I didn't feel threatened by the tiny creature.

It lingered around the pirate, unsure, then came to me and hovered just inches from my nose. My face lit up with wonder and awe when I realized that the flame was actually some kind of... fairy. It was the only word I could think to describe it. Abnormally long limbs hung from a small, round body and two almond-shaped black eyes blinked back at me. Its green glow emanated out from its figure and created a flame-like shape.

"H-hello there, little guy," I greeted and carefully brought my hand up to it. The wil-o-the-wisp looked at it and stuck out a delicate, twig-like hand to touch my finger.

"Greetings," a strange voice greeted from behind us.

The fairy's flame doused, and it zipped away into the trees. Henry and I turned, then, and found a woman standing there. Her long green skirt dragged across the ground as she ambled toward us and the torch she held lit the forest.

"Martha," Henry spoke, and I realized this was the Gaelic witch we'd been searching for. The Wil-o-the-wisp led us straight to her. I watched as he tipped his head in respect. "It's good to see you again."

"Yes," she replied, "I imagine ye've come for me help?" Her long, red hair fell in front of her as she bent to touch the torch to the ground where it lit a fire in a circle of rocks. "Good intentions, yes? Or the wisp would not have brought ye here."

Henry nodded. "Yes, good intentions. The bottle has been broken, along with the spell you cast to trap The Cobhams."

She stared at him for a moment and then turned her piercing green gaze to me. "You," she said, the English word curling on her tongue. "Ye broke the bottle?"

"Uh, yes, it was an accident."

The witch's face changed, melted into some sort of realization. "Yer not from here, Time Traveller," she said matter-of-factly and began circling the rocks toward me. Henry tensed and moved closer, shielding me with his arm.

"Dianna found the bottle in the future before she broke it. It somehow sent her back with The Cobhams," he told her.

Martha cocked her head and smiled. "The Cobhams weren't sent back, they never left, my spellbound them here, to be stuck in their *own* time." She paused and looked me up and down. "But not the bottle."

"Can you do it again?" I asked.

Martha's mouth turned into a sly grin and she sauntered back around the fire. "Aye, I can."

Henry's body relaxed. "That's excellent news. What do you—"

"I said I can. I didnae say I will," the woman replied. "Why should I help ye this time?"

Henry narrowed his gaze. "Why bring us here, then?" he asked angrily. "Just tell us what you want."

Martha's eyes shot to me and she tilted her head. "Her."

My chest tightened with panic. "Me?"

"Yes, ye don't belong here," she replied. "Ye need to go back, put things in place. Just like I told yer mother." She shook her head. "Ye Cobhams, always causing trouble."

Panic turned to shock, and my heart squeezed in my chest. "W-what did you say?"

"Oh, ye didnae know?" Martha amused. "Yer mum was a Time Traveller, too. She found herself stuck in the future when she didnae listen to me. I could feel Constance tugging at the strings of time, tryin' to find a way back. Then, one day, she stopped. I 'magine it was the day she had the likes of ye."

I shook my head, tears forcing their way from my eyes and stealing my voice. How could her words be true? Everything I ever knew replayed in my mind through a different lens. Mom. Her obsession with the past, her never-ending search for... *something*. She was trying to find a way back. My knees gave way and I fell to the ground where I wretched air from my gut.

"No, it can't be true," I cried.

"Aye, 'tis," the witch replied with certainty. Of course it was, she had no reason to lie and no way to have even known about my mom. Accepting it made more sense than denying it.

I felt Henry's hands grasp my arms and pull me back up to my feet. "Are you alright?" he whispered.

My stomach threatened to betray me, but I managed to nod. "Yes, I just can't believe it, but someh–" I stole a quick glance to the witch who swayed back and forth across the firepit, impatient, "It doesn't matter anyway, she's gone."

I didn't believe my own words and they made my throat tight to even say them. It did matter. It meant everything to me. But we had more important things to worry about. I'd process the news about my mom when this was all over when Henry and I were safe in my home in Rocky Harbour.

Martha waved her arms in an upward motion and the fire before us grew. I watched closely as she pulled a glass bottle from a green velvet bag that hung from her side.

"We must hurry. I need somethin' to lure them to us."

"Like what?" asked Henry.

"Somethin' belongin' to Maria or Eric," the witch replied and then muttered some strange words as she smoothed her hands over the bottle.

I was at a loss, but Henry turned and pinched my jacket sleeve between his fingers. It was perfect. Maria's red jacket brought me this far, it would be the thing to end it all. I nodded to him in approval.

"We have her coat," he informed the witch.

"Very well," she replied, "come and stand here." She pointed next to the fire and I followed. The three of us then formed a triangle around the blaze and the Gaelic witch continued to chant in another language. I assumed it to be Gaelic, the foreign sounds rolling off her tongue and dancing in the air around us.

"Wait," I cried out, and the two of them turned their gaze to me. "I need something first."

Martha examined my face and then nodded. "Ah, a way home."

Was she a mind reader, too? "Yes, please. Can you tell me how or give me something to send us back?"

"Us?" she asked curiously.

"For Henry and I."

"A relic I can make for ye," she answered, "but fer ye alone. Henry belongs *here*, in this time. Did ye not understand that?"

The pirate stepped closer, fists clenched at his side. "I go where Dianna goes," he insisted, "and you *will* make that happen."

"Oh, will I, now?" she challenged, eyebrows raised.

"Yes," he continued to break the triangle as he moved closer to her, "I reckon you still want to protect the boy. And you can't do that with his murderous mother burning the Earth searching for him. Dianna's jacket is the only way to locate them." He paused to let his words register with the reluctant witch. "Let us do this now, and swift. Give us a way to get to the future and we'll help you trap The Cobhams once more."

Her tense gaze shifted back and forth between Henry and I as she mulled over the deal. Finally, she responded, "Very well. But ye can't be mucking with things. Going to the future has less of an effect, but still an effect, nonetheless." She awaited our responses, but I only nodded. Martha sighed. "I'll need somethin' of yers, somethin' brought here with ye."

"You mean… from the future?" I asked and fished around in my jacket pockets for my key chain. Relief washed over me when my fingers found it. "Here, this should work." I walked around the fire and placed the snow globe in her hand.

She held it up and examined it curiously before cupping her hands around it. I watched intently as Martha closed her eyes and mumbled a Gaelic chant. She bent down to pinch some earth between her fingers and sprinkled it over the trinket. A red light began to seep from the cracks between her fingers and the fire grew next to me.

Henry took the moment to reach out and hold my hand. He brought it up to his lips and placed a gentle kiss across my fingers. "Are you truly alright?"

I managed a deep and shaky breath. "Yes, I'll be fine."

"But your mother–"

"I'll be fine," I said again and then added, "eventually." Henry responded with a light squeeze of my hand and I stepped closer to kiss his face. "I'll have you to get me through it."

Finally, she stopped, and her eyes flew open. "There," she handed the key chain, now warm to the touch, back to me, "when yer ready, simply break the relic and ye will find yerself back home." She stole a sly glance toward Henry and then quickly darted back to me. "Be sure yer touching him when ye do, or he won't be travelin' anywhere."

I beamed and clutched the snow globe tightly before returning it to my pocket. "Thank you." Her only response was a defiant harrumph and I took my place in the triangle once again.

"The bottle is prepared," she called out to us as the fire crackled loudly in the center. "We just need to draw them near. Are ye ready?"

Henry and I exchanged looks and then nodded.

"Hold out yer arms," she instructed, "and do not break the circle, no matter what. The spell will cease."

I swallowed hard against my suddenly dry throat but held my stance around the fire. Martha's eyes closed as she chanted away, spewing words I couldn't understand. The fire came to life and danced before us, casting shadows on the trees and forest floor. Henry and I stared at one another, unable to touch, but comforting each other the only way we could. I saw the fierceness to protect me in his black eyes, and I willed him to be okay. We stood and listened to Martha chant and taunt the fire with her magic for a good while, and I began to worry that it wasn't working. Was it possible that The Cobhams had already fled the area? Were they too far away for the effects of the spell to take hold?

Suddenly, a shadow caught my eye, only because it was out of place. It didn't dance with the flames. I narrowed my gaze and focused on two dark figures, making their way through the trees behind Henry.

Adrenaline coursed through my veins and my lungs strained to take a deep breath, but my heart pumped too fast to allow it. This was it. This was the moment I hoped never had to happen. The moment when I'd actually meet the devil woman. The tall, feminine figure stepped out from the treeline and our fire lit her features. My body raced with heat; fear and adrenaline coursing through me like molten glass.

There she was.

Maria Lindsay Cobham. In the flesh.

Eric soon sidled up next to her and they both looked around in confusion, swords drawn. Her eyes landed on the witch and Maria lunged.

"You!" she spat loudly. "You wretched sorceress. Where is my son?"

"Maria, look," Eric spoke and pointed to the now glowing glass bottle at Martha's feet.

The witch didn't even open her eyes or break from her chant.

But Henry spoke. "Step away from her, Maria."

The woman turned her crazed face toward Henry and it washed over with devilish delight. Her hips swayed, and she danced toward my pirate.

"Pet," she cooed, and my stomach rolled, "So, you live, do you?"

Maria motioned for Eric to stay with the witch and he brought his sword to Martha's throat. Then I watched as her hands smoothed over Henry's shoulders and pure rage filled my body. I nearly jumped after her, but the witch's magic held me in place, told me not to budge. It killed me to watch, but I couldn't tear my eyes away. If she hurt him, I would end her life.

My lineage be damned.

Bile rose in my throat as Maria's lips brushed Henry's ear and I heard her say, "My pet, why did you leave me? You don't love me anymore?"

"You haven't the faintest idea what love is," Henry replied through clenched teeth. It hurt him to have her hands on his body, I could see the pain in his tortured face. "You're a poison upon this Earth."

Her expression turned into a mock frown. "Aww, now you don't mean that, do ya, Pet?" she continued to smooth his shoulders, his face, while her head cocked from side to side, examining him like a vulture. "I spent years cursing your name, but freedom tastes so good." Her face tipped up toward the sky and I saw her eyes roll back like a junkie breathing in the scent of their beloved drug. "I can forgive you for abandoning me." I watched her pull a small dagger from her side and lightly drag it across the skin of his neck. He flinched as blood drew from the wound and she stared at it with crazed delight. "Oh, how I miss the way you bleed."

"Get your hands off him!" I yelled, no longer able to remain silent. Henry was mine, and mine alone.

Her head of black curls snapped to attention and whipped around to find me standing in my corner. Her eyes, more black and devilish than Henry's ever were, burned into me.

"And what do we have here?"

"Henry is *mine*," I told her.

With her sword lifted waist high, Maria Lindsay Cobham took careful steps toward me, her big brown boots crunching the forest floor beneath her. The tip of her sword pricked the shoulder of my coat and lightly dragged down to its bottom hem.

"That," she spoke angrily, "is *my* jacket." Suddenly, the pointy tip flew up to my throat. "I should cut it from your body."

"Maria!" Henry bellowed from over her shoulder, and I watched the woman's mouth twist into a sick grin. She was just trying to get a reaction from him. And it was working.

Maria moved like a snake and came to stand behind me, her sword raised and placed across my throat as her free hand reached around and rested on my stomach. "Stop the ritual right now or I'll gut her like a rotten fish."

"Henry don't," I pleaded.

His body shook with anger as he fought to not break the triangle. The Gaelic witch still muttered her chants, despite being held at knifepoint by Maria's husband, and the fire blazed before us as wisps of green and red light danced through the circle like colorful spirits.

"I'm not worth it. They need to be stopped. Think of the lives you can save."

He cringed. "Yours is the only one that matters to me." He looked to Eric, who still held a sword to the witch's neck, and then back to us. "What do you expect me to do, Dianna?"

"Nothing, Captain," a voice spoke from the trees. Its sound filled me with hope and I risked searching for it. Finn, Gus, and Charlie emerged from the woods, pistols pointed at The Cobhams. "Stay right where ye are."

Finn and Charlie came toward me while Gus unarmed Eric. But Henry still appeared shaken. "Do not shoot to kill, they must be kept alive," he ordered. Yes, they couldn't die, or I would disintegrate into time.

"Aye, Captain," Finn answered. "We caught sight of the two devils and followed them through the forest. Good thing, too." But the second his back turned, Maria released me and grabbed a hold of young Charlie.

"No!" I screamed and broke the triangle to lunge toward them. But Maria began to back away with Charlie held tightly in her grasp.

"Come near me and you'll be down one man," she spat. "Drop your pistols."

"No," Charlie shouted, "Don't do it."

I couldn't take my eyes from his sweet, terrified face. His words told us not to, but his eyes begged to be saved. I wanted nothing more to rip him from her wretched hold, my sweet Charlie. How dare she lay hands on him. I craned my head to catch the men slowly lay their pistols down and then turned back to Maria who sported a dark and twisted grin.

Then, everything seemed to happen in slow motion, even though my body forced itself against the blanket of time around us, I couldn't move fast enough to save him. I watched as Maria's silver blade caught the light of the fire and sliced through young Charlie's neck, blood spewed and fell to the forest floor.

She let his corpse crumble at her feet and flung her blade again, toward me, its thick edge catching my upper shoulder. The force of her thrust and the sudden pain knocked me back and I fell to the ground where I heard the crushing sound of hard plastic breaking. My eyes widened in horror when I realized what the sound was.

The snow globe. My ticket home.

I accidentally cashed it in and I felt the threads of time beginning to pull me into oblivion.

"No!" I screamed again as I reached out for Henry.

But it was too late. The last image I took with me was that of my beloved, eyes bulging, his mouth gaped from screaming as he clawed his way toward me, and the hands of everyone around covered his body, pulling him away.

And then there was darkness.

THE END

C ontinue the epic tale of Henry and Dianna's adventure with book two in The Dark Tides Trilogy, **The Pirate Queen**, available wherever books are sold!

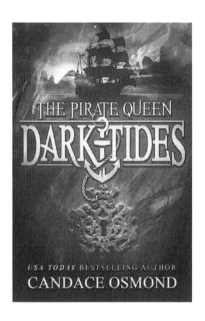

ABOUT THE AUTHOR

#1 International and *USA TODAY* Bestselling Author, Candace Osmond was born in North York, ON. She published her first book by the age of 25, the first installment in a Paranormal Romance Trilogy called The Iron World Series.
Candace is also one of the creative writers for sssh.com, an acclaimed Erotic Romance website for women which has been featured on NBC Nightline and a number of other large platforms like Cosmo. Her most recent project is a screen play that received a nomination for an AVN Award. Now residing in a small town in Newfoundland with her husband and two kids, Candace writes full time developing articles for just about every niche, more novels, and a hoard of short stories.

Connect with Candace online! She LOVES to hear from readers! *www.AuthorCandaceOsmond.com*

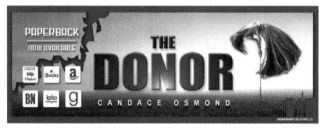

Made in the USA
Middletown, DE
20 August 2021

46484211R00137